Shudders

TEN STRANGE JOURNEYS INTO THE UNKNOWN

Great tales of suspense and terror written by masters of the macabre. . . .

Heart-trembling reports from the uncanny world of witches, warlocks, and demons. . . .

Ten stories of unexplained events and unholy beings, calculated to give you the

SHUDDERS

TEN TALES
CALCULATED
TO GIVE YOU

Shudders

edited by ROSS R. OLNEY

cover by HAL FRENCK

GOLDEN PRESS
Western Publishing Company, Inc.
Racine, Wisconsin

The publisher has made every effort to trace the ownership of all copyrighted material and to secure permission from the holders of such rights. In the event of any question arising as to the use of any material, the publisher, while expressing regret for inadvertent error, will be pleased to make the necessary correction in future printings.

ACKNOWLEDGMENTS

"The Waxwork" by A. M. Burrage, from *Someone in the Room* by Ex-Private X. Reprinted by permission of Jarrolds Publishers (London) Ltd.

"The Inexperienced Ghost" by H. G. Wells, from *The Short Stories of H. G. Wells.* Reprinted by permission of the Executors of the Estate of H. G. Wells.

"Sweets to the Sweet," by Robert Bloch, copyright 1947 by *Weird Tales;* copyright 1960 by Robert Bloch. By permission of Arkham House.

"Used Car," by H. Russell Wakefield, copyright 1946 by H. Russell Wakefield. By permission of Arkham House.

"The Last Drive," by Carl Jacobi, copyright 1933 by the Popular Fiction Publishing Company; copyright 1947 by Carl Jacobi. By permission of Arkham House.

"Second Night Out," by Frank Belknap Long, copyright 1933 by the Popular Fiction Publishing Company; copyright 1946 by Frank Belknap Long. By permission of Arkham House.

"The Whistling Room," by William Hope Hodgson, copyright 1909, 1910 by William Hope Hodgson; copyright 1947 by August Derleth. By permission of Arkham House.

"The Hills Beyond Furcy" by Robert G. Anderson, © 1966 by H. S. D. Publications, Inc. Reprinted by permission of the author and Larry Sternig Literary Agency. Story originally appeared in the March, 1966, issue of *Alfred Hitchcock's Mystery Magazine.*

"Floral Tribute" by Robert Bloch. Copyright 1949 by *Weird Tales.* Reprinted by permission of the author. Story originally published in July, 1949, *Weird Tales.*

"The Monkey's Paw" by W. W. Jacobs. Reprinted with the permission of The Society of Authors as the literary representative of the Estate of W. W. Jacobs.

TABLE OF CONTENTS

A Forewarning

Doors locked?

Windows securely barred?

In these pages you are going to encounter some strange, eerie events, meet some highly unusual beings, and learn of many weird things that happen, even to ordinary people like you and me.

Of course, locking up does create a problem. When you hear that unexpected noise in the next room or the breathing just behind your chair, you will know at once that no *human* could have entered through your locks and your bars.

What else could be causing the frightening sounds? If you don't know yet, you will after reading these stories from the masters. They know well, and herein they will tell you.

Pretty little Irma, for instance, didn't look at all like a witch—or so says ghost expert Robert Bloch. But in the chilling "Sweets to the Sweet" you will learn that she was by no means an ordinary little girl. Her father learned, too, but in a horrible, horrible way.

How often have you joked about spending the night in an empty old house with a reputation for being haunted, or in a cemetery, where the very silence seems to scream out at midnight? In "The Waxwork" by A. M. Burrage, a poor journalist who needs the money agrees to spend a night in the Murderers' Den. Of course, the figures lurking in the shadows all around are only wax—or are they?

You may not want to ride in an automobile again after reading H. R. Wakefield's bizarre "Used Car." Certainly it's ridiculous even to imagine that such things could happen in this modern day and age, but chances are you'll still be thinking of Wakefield's used car the next time you climb into the family sedan—especially if there happens to be an odd stain on the upholstery.

Did you ever meet a ghost? Face-to-face, that is, where you could chat with him, and where he would answer your questions? Probably not; most of us have not been that "lucky." But H. G. Wells's hero did in "The Inexperienced Ghost," even if this was a ghost like none you ever imagined before. This was an unhappy, confused specter, who only wanted to return to his ghostly domain. The problem was that, in so doing, he revealed some ghostly secrets to mortal men.

For sheer terror, "The Whistling Room" by William Hope Hodgson must rate high on the list. It was Carnacki's job to find and drive away the evil spirits, but the spirits in this horrid room gave the expert his greatest challenge. For this one you will most certainly want the doors and windows locked, and even then you will wonder if you have done the wise thing, after all.

Jeb Waters was a truck driver who only wanted to deliver his cargo from the railhead at Littleton to the town of Marchester. It was a routine job, under normal circumstances. But this was a night of bitter cold and driving snow, and there was the cargo to consider— not that the freezing cold would have any effect on the coffin or its contents. Poor, terrified Jeb, insane with fear of . . . of what? You'll find out in "The Last Drive" by Carl Jacobi.

One of the great masterpieces of terror is W. W. Jacobs' story "The Monkey's Paw." What would you do if you could make three wishes and be certain they would come true? Would you stop and think about it, or would you blindly call out for your fondest desires? This poor couple had no idea that what they were asking of the gnarled, ugly little paw would bring a scream of pure horror to their lips—and to the hearts of everyone hearing the story ever since.

How about a relaxing ocean cruise? Wonderful, just so you don't make the voyage on Frank Belknap Long's terror ship in "Second Night Out." And, whatever ship you make the trip on, beware of an overpowering stench that assaults the nostrils and flip-flops the stomach, for you could be in the presence of Long's hideous creature—and it could be seeking you.

Roger saw the power of Tienne with his own eyes in Bob Anderson's "The Hills Beyond Furcy," and he also saw the deep feeling Tienne held for Carol. Yet Roger still took his lovely young bride to Port-au-Prince for their honeymoon. Port-au-Prince was Tienne's own home ground, where weird voodoo rites were a way of life rather than a bit of entertainment at a cocktail party. And Tienne wanted Carol desperately. . . .

Still, in "Floral Tribute," Bob Bloch's final offering, we learn that ghosts are not necessarily evil. They can, in fact, be good friends to mortals. They ask only that you believe in their existence, that you do not scoff, that you meet them as equals, though you live in different worlds. Yes, they can be good and true friends, even to the point of seeing that you repay their visit—and come to live with them!

A Forewarning

Doors locked? Windows barred?

Perhaps you shouldn't waste your time on these symbols of human vulnerability, after all. As you read your way through this collection of notable ghost stories, you'll learn that locks and bars mean very little to these beings.

If they want to reach you, they will.

ROSS R. OLNEY

ROBERT BLOCH

Sweets to the Sweet

Irma didn't look like a witch.

She had small, regular features, a peaches-and-cream complexion, blue eyes, and fair, almost ash-blond hair. Besides, she was only eight years old.

"Why does he tease her so?" sobbed Miss Pall. "That's where she got the idea in the first place—because he always insists on calling her a little witch."

Sam Steever bulked his paunch back into the squeaky swivel chair and folded his heavy hands in his lap.

His fat lawyer's mask was immobile, but he was really quite distressed.

Women like Miss Pall should never sob. Their glasses wiggle, their thin noses twitch, their creasy eyelids redden, and their stringy hair becomes disarrayed.

"Please, control yourself," coaxed Sam Steever. "Perhaps if we could just talk this whole thing over sensibly—"

"I don't care!" Miss Pall sniffled. "I'm not going back there again. I can't stand it. There's nothing I can do, anyway. The man is your brother, and she's your brother's child. It's not my responsibility. I've tried—"

"Of course you've tried." Sam Steever smiled benignly, as if Miss Pall were foreman of a jury. "I quite understand. But I still don't see why you are so upset, dear lady."

Miss Pall removed her spectacles and dabbed at her eyes with a floral-print handkerchief. Then she deposited the soggy ball in her purse, snapped the catch, replaced her spectacles, and sat up straight.

"Very well, Mr. Steever," she said. "I shall do my best to acquaint you with my reasons for quitting your brother's employ."

She suppressed a tardy sniff.

"I came to John Steever two years ago in response to an advertisement for a housekeeper, as you know. When I found that I was to be governess to a motherless six-year-old child, I was at first distressed. I knew nothing of the care of children."

"John had a nurse the first six years." Sam Steever nodded. "You know Irma's mother died in childbirth."

"I am aware of that," said Miss Pall primly. "Naturally, one's heart goes out to a lonely, neglected little girl. And she was so terribly lonely, Mr. Steever—if you could have seen her, moping around in the corners of that big, ugly old house—"

"I have seen her," said Sam Steever hastily, hoping to forestall another outburst. "And I know what you've done for Irma. My brother is inclined to be thoughtless, even a bit selfish, at times. He doesn't understand."

"He's cruel!" declared Miss Pall, suddenly vehement. "Cruel and wicked. Even if he is your brother, I say he's no fit father for any child. When I came there, her little arms were black-and-blue from beatings. He used to take a belt—"

"I know. Sometimes I think John never recovered from the shock of Mrs. Steever's death. That's why I was so pleased when you came, dear lady. I thought you might help improve the situation."

"I tried," Miss Pall whimpered. "You know I tried. I never raised a hand to that child in two years, though many's the time your brother told me to punish her. 'Give the little witch a beating,' he used to say. 'That's all she needs—a good thrashing.' And then she'd hide behind my back and whisper to me to protect her. But she wouldn't cry, Mr. Steever. Do you know, I've never seen her cry."

21

Sam Steever felt vaguely irritated and a bit bored. He wished the old hen would get on with it. So he smiled and oozed treacle.

"But just what exactly is your problem, dear lady?"

"Everything was all right when I came there. We got along just splendidly. I started to teach Irma to read—and was surprised to find that she had already mastered reading. Your brother disclaimed having taught her, but she spent hours curled up on the sofa with a book. 'Just like her,' he used to say. 'Unnatural little witch. Doesn't play with the other children. Little witch.'

"That's just the way he kept talking, Mr. Steever. As if she were some sort of . . . I don't know what. And she so sweet and quiet and pretty!

"Is it any wonder she read? I used to be that way myself when I was a girl, because— But never mind.

"Still, it was a shock that day I found her looking through the *Encyclopaedia Britannica.* 'What are you reading, Irma?' I asked her. And she showed me. It was the article on witchcraft.

"You see what morbid thoughts your brother has inculcated in her poor little head?

"I did my best. I went out and bought her

some toys—she had absolutely nothing, you know, not even a doll. She didn't even know how to *play!* I tried to get her interested in some of the other little girls in the neighborhood, but it was no use. They didn't understand her, and she didn't understand them. There were scenes. Children can be cruel, thoughtless. And her father wouldn't let her go to public school. I was to teach her.

"Then I brought her the modeling clay. She liked that. She would spend hours just making faces with clay. For a child of six, Irma displayed real talent.

"We made little dolls together, and I sewed clothes for them. That first year was a happy one, Mr. Steever. Particularly during those months when your brother was away in South America. But this year, when he came back— oh, I can't bear to talk about it!"

"Please," said Sam Steever. "You must understand. John is not a happy man. The loss of his wife, the decline of his import trade, and his drinking—but you know all that."

"All I know is that he hates Irma," snapped Miss Pall suddenly. "He hates her. He wants her to be bad so he can whip her. 'If you don't discipline the little witch, I shall,' he always says. And then he takes her upstairs and thrashes her with his belt. You must do something, Mr.

23

Steever, you must—or I'll go to the authorities myself."

The crazy old biddy would, at that, Sam Steever thought. Remedy—more treacle. "But about Irma," he persisted.

"She's changed, too. Ever since her father returned this year. She won't play with me anymore. Hardly looks at me. It's as though I failed her, Mr. Steever, in not protecting her from that man. Besides—she thinks she's a witch."

Crazy. Stark, staring crazy. Sam Steever creaked upright in his chair.

"Oh, you needn't look at me like that, Mr. Steever. She'd tell you so herself—if you ever visited the house!"

He caught the reproach in her voice and assuaged it with a deprecating nod.

"She told me, all right: If her father wants her to be a witch, she'll be a witch. And she won't play with me or anyone else, because witches don't play. Last Halloween she wanted me to give her a broomstick. Oh, it would be funny if it weren't so tragic.

"Just a few weeks ago, I thought she'd changed. That's when she asked me to take her to church one Sunday. 'I want to see the baptism,' she said. Imagine that—an eight-year-old interested in baptism! Reading too much, that's what does it.

24

"Well, we went to church, and she was as sweet as can be, wearing her new blue dress and holding my hand. I was proud of her, Mr. Steever, really proud.

"But after that, she went right back into her shell. Reading around the house, running through the yard at twilight, talking to herself.

"Perhaps it's because your brother wouldn't bring her a kitten. She was pestering him for a black cat, and he asked why, and she said, 'Because witches always have black cats.' Then he took her upstairs.

"I can't stop him, you know. He beat her again the night the power failed and we couldn't find the candles. He said she'd stolen them. Imagine that—accusing an eight-year-old child of stealing candles!

"That was the beginning of the end. Then today, when he found his hairbrush missing—"

"You say he beat her with his hairbrush?"

"Yes. She admitted having stolen it. Said she wanted it for her doll."

"But didn't you say she has no dolls?"

"She made one. At least, I think she did. I've never seen it. She won't show us anything anymore; won't talk to us at table. It's just impossible to handle her.

"But this doll she made—it's a small one, I know, because at times she carries it tucked under her arm. She talks to it and pets it, but she won't show it to me or to him. He asked her about the hairbrush, and she said she took it for the doll.

"Your brother flew into a terrible rage—he'd been drinking in his room again all morning; don't think I don't know it!—and she just smiled and said he could have it now. She went over to her bureau and handed it to him. She hadn't harmed it in the least; his hair was still in it, I noticed.

"But he snatched it up, and then he started to strike her about the shoulders with it, and he twisted her arm, and then he—"

Miss Pall huddled in her chair and summoned great racking sobs from her thin chest.

Sam Steever patted her shoulder, fussing about her like an elephant over a wounded canary.

"That's all, Mr. Steever. I came right to you. I'm not even going back to that house to get my things. I can't stand any more—the way he beat her—and the way she didn't cry, but just giggled and giggled and giggled. Sometimes I think she *is* a witch—that he made her into a witch. . . ."

Sam Steever picked up the phone. The ringing had broken the relief of silence after Miss

Pall's hasty and not unwelcome departure.

"Hello—that you, Sam?"

He recognized his brother's voice, somewhat the worse for drink.

"Yes, John."

"I suppose the old bat came running straight to you to shoot her mouth off."

"If you mean Miss Pall, I've seen her, yes."

"Pay no attention to her. I can explain everything."

"Do you want me to stop in? I haven't paid you a visit in months."

"Well—not right now. Got an appointment with the doctor this evening."

"Something wrong?"

"Pain in my arm. Rheumatism or something. Getting a little diathermy. But I'll call you tomorrow, and we'll straighten this whole mess out."

"Right."

But John Steever did not call his brother the next day. Along about suppertime, Sam called him.

Surprisingly enough, Irma answered the phone.

Her thin, squeaky little voice sounded faintly in Sam's ear.

"Daddy's upstairs sleeping," she said. "He's been sick."

"Well, don't disturb him. What is it—his arm?"

"His back, now. He has to go to the doctor again in a little while."

"Tell him I'll call tomorrow, then. Uh—everything all right, Irma? I mean, don't you miss Miss Pall?"

"No. I'm glad she went away. She's stupid."

"Oh. Yes. I see. But you phone me if you want anything. And I hope your daddy's better."

"Yes. So do I," said Irma. Then she began to giggle, and then she hung up.

There was no giggling the following afternoon when John Steever called Sam at the office. His voice was sober—with the sharp sobriety of pain.

"Sam—for the love of heaven, get over here. Something's happening to me!"

"What's the trouble?"

"The pain—it's killing me! I've got to see you. Quickly!"

"There's a client in the office, but I'll get rid of him. Say, wait a minute. Why don't you call the doctor?"

"That quack can't help me. He gave me diathermy for my arm, and yesterday he did the same thing for my back."

"Didn't it help?"

"The pain went away, yes. But it's back now.

I feel . . . as if I'm being crushed. Squeezed, here in the chest. I can't breathe."

"Sounds like pleurisy. Why don't you call him?"

"It isn't pleurisy. He examined me. Said I was sound as a dollar. No, there's nothing organically wrong. And I couldn't tell him the real cause."

"Real cause?"

"Yes. The pins. The pins that little fiend is sticking into the doll she made. Into the arm, the back. And now heaven only knows how she's causing *this*."

"John, you mustn't—"

"Oh, what's the use of talking? I can't move off the bed here. She has me now. I can't go down and stop her, get hold of the doll. And nobody else would believe it. But it's the doll, all right, the one she made with the candle wax and the hair from my brush. Oh—it hurts to talk—that cursed little witch! Hurry, Sam. Promise me you'll do something—anything to get that doll from her—get that doll—"

Half an hour later, at four-thirty, Sam Steever entered his brother's house.

Irma opened the door.

It gave Sam a shock to see her standing there, smiling and unperturbed, pale blond hair

29

brushed immaculately back from the rosy oval of her face. She looked just like a little doll. A little doll—

"Hello, Uncle Sam."

"Hello, Irma. Your daddy called me; did he tell you? He said he wasn't feeling well—"

"Yes, I know. But he's all right now. He's sleeping."

Something happened to Sam Steever; a drop of ice water trickled down his spine.

"Sleeping?" he croaked. "Upstairs?"

Before she opened her mouth to answer, he was bounding up the steps to the second floor and striding down the hall to his brother John's bedroom.

John lay on the bed. He was asleep—only asleep. Sam Steever noted the regular rise and fall of his chest as he breathed. His face was calm, relaxed.

Then the drop of ice water evaporated, and Sam could afford to smile—and even to murmur, "Nonsense!" under his breath as he turned away.

As he went downstairs, he hastily improvised plans. A six-month vacation for his brother; avoid calling it a "cure." An orphanage for Irma; give her a chance to get away from this morbid old house, all those books. . . .

He paused halfway down the stairs. Peering

over the banister through the twilight, he saw Irma on the sofa, cuddled up like a little white ball. She was talking to something she cradled in her arms, rocking it to and fro.

Then there was a doll, after all.

Sam Steever tiptoed very quietly down the stairs and walked over to Irma.

"Hello," he said.

She jumped. Both arms rose to cover completely whatever it was she had been fondling. She squeezed it tightly.

Sam Steever thought of a doll being squeezed across the chest. . . .

Irma stared up at him, her face a mask of innocence. In the half-light her face did resemble a mask. The mask of a little girl, covering —what?

"Daddy's better now, isn't he?" lisped Irma.

"Yes, much better."

"I knew he would be."

"But I'm afraid he's going to have to go away for a rest—a long rest."

A smile filtered through the mask. "Good," said Irma.

"Of course," Sam went on, "you couldn't stay here all alone. I was wondering—maybe we could send you off to school or to some kind of home—"

Irma giggled. "Oh, you needn't worry about

31

me," she said. She shifted about on the sofa as Sam sat down, then sprang up quickly as he came close to her.

Her arms shifted with the movement, and Sam Steever saw a pair of tiny legs dangling below her elbow. There were trousers on the legs, and little bits of leather for shoes.

"What's that you have, Irma?" he asked. "Is it a doll?"

Slowly he extended his pudgy hand.

She pulled back.

"You can't see it," she said.

"But I want to. Miss Pall said you made such lovely ones."

"Miss Pall is stupid. So are you," Irma said. "Go away."

"Please, Irma. Let me see it."

But even as he spoke, Sam Steever was staring at the top of the doll, momentarily revealed when she backed away. It was a head, all right, with wisps of hair over a white face. Dusk dimmed the features, but Sam recognized the eyes, the nose, the chin.

He could keep up the pretense no longer.

"Give me that doll, Irma!" he snapped. "I know what it is. I know *who* it is—"

For an instant, the mask slipped from Irma's face, and Sam Steever stared into naked fear.

She knew. She knew he knew.

Then, just as quickly, the mask was replaced.

Irma was only a sweet, spoiled, stubborn little girl as she shook her head merrily and smiled with impish mischief in her eyes.

"Oh, Uncle Sam," she giggled, "you're so silly! Why, this isn't a *real* doll."

"What is it, then?" he muttered.

Irma giggled once more, raising the figure as she spoke. "Why, it's only—candy!" she said.

"Candy?"

Irma nodded. Then, very swiftly, she slipped the tiny head of the image into her mouth.

And bit it off.

There was a single piercing scream from up-stairs.

As Sam Steever turned and ran up the steps, little Irma, still gravely munching, skipped out of the front door and into the night beyond.

A. M. BURRAGE

The Waxwork

While the uniformed attendants of Marriner's Waxworks were ushering the last stragglers through the great glass-paneled double doors, the manager sat in his office interviewing Raymond Hewson.

The manager was a youngish man, stout, blond, and of medium height. He wore his clothes well and contrived to look extremely smart without appearing overdressed. Raymond Hewson looked neither. His clothes, which had been good when new and which were still carefully brushed and pressed, were beginning to show signs of their owner's losing battle with the world. He was a small, spare, pale man, with lank, errant brown hair, and, although he spoke plausibly and even forcibly, he had the defensive and somewhat furtive air of a man who was used to rebuffs. He looked what he was: a man gifted somewhat above the ordinary, who was a failure through his lack of self-assertion.

The manager was speaking.

"There is nothing new in your request," he said. "In fact, we refuse it to different people— mostly young bloods who have tried to make bets—about three times a week. We have nothing to gain and something to lose by letting people spend the night in our Murderers' Den. If I allowed it, and some young idiot lost his senses, what would be my position? But your being a journalist somewhat alters the case."

Hewson smiled.

"I suppose you mean that journalists have no senses to lose."

"No, no," laughed the manager, "but one imagines them to be responsible people. Besides, here we have something to gain: publicity and advertisement."

"Exactly," said Hewson, "and there I thought we might come to terms."

The manager laughed again. "Oh," he exclaimed, "I know what's coming! You want to be paid twice, do you? It used to be said years ago that Madame Tussaud's would give a man a hundred pounds for sleeping alone in the Chamber of Horrors. I hope you don't think that we have made any such offer. Er—what is your paper, Mr. Hewson?"

"I am free-lancing at present," Hewson confessed, "working on space for several papers.

However, I should find no difficulty in getting the story printed. The *Morning Echo* would use it like a shot. 'A Night with Marriner's Murderers.' No live paper could turn it down.''

The manager rubbed his chin. ''Ah! And how do you propose to treat it?''

''I shall make it gruesome, of course; gruesome, with just a saving touch of humor.''

The other nodded and offered Hewson his cigarette case. ''Very well, Mr. Hewson,'' he said. ''Get your story printed in the *Morning Echo*, and there will be a five-pound note waiting for you here when you care to come and call for it. But, first of all, it's no small ordeal that you're proposing to undertake. I'd like to be quite sure about you, and I'd like you to be sure about yourself. I must own I shouldn't care to take it on. I've seen those figures dressed and undressed, I know all about the process of their manufacture, I can walk about in company downstairs as unmoved as if I were walking among so many skittles, but I should hate having to sleep down there alone among them.''

''Why?'' asked Hewson.

''I don't know. There isn't any reason. I don't believe in ghosts. If I did, I should expect them to haunt the scene of their crimes or the spot where their bodies were laid, instead of a cellar that happens to contain their waxwork effigies. It's just that I couldn't sit alone among them all night, with their seeming to stare at me in the way they do. After all, they represent the lowest and most appalling types of humanity, and—although I would not own it publicly —the people who come to see them are not generally charged with the very highest motives. The whole atmosphere of the place is unpleasant, and if you are susceptible to atmosphere, I warn you that you are in for a very uncomfortable night."

Hewson had known that from the moment when the idea had first occurred to him. His soul sickened at the prospect, even while he smiled casually upon the manager. But he had a wife and family to keep, and for the past month he had been living on paragraphs, eked out by his rapidly dwindling store of savings. Here was a chance not to be missed—the price of a special story in the *Morning Echo*, with a five-pound note to add to it. It meant comparative wealth and luxury for a week and freedom from the worst anxieties for a fortnight. Besides, if he wrote the story well, it might lead to an offer of regular employment.

"The way of transgressors—and newspapermen—is hard," he said. "I have already promised myself an uncomfortable night, because your Murderers' Den is obviously not fitted up

37

as a hotel bedroom. But I don't think your wax-works will worry me much."

"You're not superstitious?"

"Not a bit." Hewson laughed.

"But you're a journalist; you must have a strong imagination."

"The news editors for whom I've worked have always complained that I haven't any. Plain facts are not considered sufficient in our trade, and the papers don't like offering their readers unbuttered bread."

The manager smiled and rose. "Right," he said. "I think the last of the people have gone. Wait a moment. I'll give orders for the figures downstairs not to be draped, and let the night people know that you'll be here. Then I'll take you down and show you round."

He picked up the receiver of a house telephone, spoke into it, and presently replaced it. "One condition I'm afraid I must impose on you," he remarked. "I must ask you not to smoke. We had a fire scare down in the Murderers' Den this evening. I don't know who gave the alarm, but, whoever it was, it was a false one. Fortunately there were very few people down there at the time, or there might have been a panic. And now, if you're ready, we'll make a move."

Hewson followed the manager through half

a dozen rooms, where attendants were busy shrouding the kings and queens of England, the generals and prominent statesmen of this and other generations, all the mixed herd of humanity whose fame or notoriety had rendered them eligible for this kind of immortality. The manager stopped once and spoke to a man in uniform, saying something about an armchair in the Murderers' Den.

"It's the best we can do for you, I'm afraid," he said to Hewson. "I hope you'll be able to get some sleep."

He led the way through an open barrier and down ill-lit stone stairs that conveyed a sinister impression of giving access to a dungeon. In a passage at the bottom were a few preliminary horrors, such as relics of the Inquisition, a rack taken from a medieval castle, branding irons, thumbscrews, and other mementos of man's onetime cruelty to man. Beyond the passage was the Murderers' Den.

It was a room of irregular shape, with a vaulted roof, dimly lit by electric lights burning behind inverted bowls of frosted glass. It was, by design, an eerie and uncomfortable chamber —a chamber whose atmosphere invited its visitors to speak in whispers. There was something of the air of a chapel about it, but a chapel no longer devoted to the practice of piety and given over now for base and impious worship.

The waxwork murderers stood on low pedestals, with numbered tickets at their feet. Seeing them elsewhere, and without knowing whom they represented, one would have thought them a dull-looking crew, chiefly remarkable for the shabbiness of their clothes and as evidence of the changes in fashion even among the unfashionable.

Recent notorieties rubbed dusty shoulders with the old "favorites." Thurtell, the murderer of Weir, stood as if frozen in the act of making a shopwindow gesture to young Bywaters. There was Lefroy, the poor half-baked little snob who killed for gain so that he might ape the gentleman. Within five yards of him sat Mrs. Thompson, that erotic romanticist, hanged to propitiate British middle-class matronhood. Charles Peace, the only member of that vile company who looked uncompromisingly and entirely evil, sneered across a gangway at Norman Thorne. Browne and Kennedy, the two most recent additions, stood between Mrs. Dyer and Patrick Mahon.

The manager, walking around with Hewson, pointed out several of the more interesting of these unholy notabilities. "That's Crippen; I expect you recognize him. Insignificant little beast who looks as if he couldn't tread on a worm.

That's Armstrong. Looks like a decent, harmless country gentleman, doesn't he? There's old Vaquier; you can't miss him because of his beard. And, of course, this—"

"Who's that?" Hewson interrupted in a whisper, pointing.

"Oh, I was coming to him," said the manager, in a light undertone. "Come and have a good look at him. This is our star turn. He's the only one of the bunch that hasn't been hanged."

The figure that Hewson had indicated was that of a small, slight man, not much more than five feet in height. It wore little waxed mustaches, large spectacles, and a caped coat. There was something so exaggeratedly French in its appearance that it reminded Hewson of a stage caricature. He could not have said precisely why the mild-looking face seemed to him so repellent, but he had already recoiled a step, and, even in the manager's company, it cost him an effort to look again.

"But who is he?" he asked.

"That," said the manager, "is Dr. Bourdette."

Hewson shook his head doubtfully. "I think I've heard the name," he said, "but I forget in connection with what."

The manager smiled. "You'd remember better if you were a Frenchman," he said. "For some long while that man was the terror of Paris. He carried on his work of healing by day, and of throat-cutting by night, when the fit was on him. He killed for the sheer devilish pleasure it gave him to kill, and always in the same way—with a razor. After his last crime, he left a clue behind him that set the police upon his track. One clue led to another, and before very long, they knew that they were on the track of the Parisian equivalent of our Jack the Ripper and had enough evidence to send him to the mad-house or the guillotine on a dozen capital charges.

"But even then our friend here was too clever for them. When he realized that the toils were closing about him, he mysteriously disappeared, and ever since, the police of every civilized country have been looking for him. There is no doubt that he managed to make away with himself, and by some means that has prevented his body's coming to light. One or two crimes of a similar nature have taken place since his disappearance, but he is believed almost for certain to be dead, and the experts believe these recrudescences to be the work of an imitator. It's queer, isn't it, how every notorious murderer has imitators?"

Hewson shuddered and fidgeted with his feet. "I don't like him at all," he confessed. "Ugh! What eyes he's got!"

"Yes, this figure's a little masterpiece. You find the eyes bite into you? Well, that's excellent realism, then, for Bourdette practised mesmerism and was supposed to mesmerize his victims before dispatching them. Indeed, had he not done so, it is impossible to see how so small a man could have done his ghastly work. There were never any signs of a struggle."

"I thought I saw him move," said Hewson, with a catch in his voice.

The manager smiled. "You'll have more than one optical illusion before the night's out, I expect. You shan't be locked in. You can come upstairs when you've had enough of it. There are watchmen on the premises, so you'll find company. Don't be alarmed if you hear them moving about. I'm sorry I can't give you any more light, because all the lights are on. For obvious reasons, we keep this place as gloomy as possible. And now I think you had better return with me to the office and have a tot of whisky before beginning your night's vigil."

The member of the night staff who placed the armchair for Hewson was inclined to be facetious.

"Where will you have it, sir?" he asked, grinning. "Just 'ere, so as you can 'ave a little talk with Crippen when you're tired of sitting still?

Or there's old Mother Dyer over there, making eyes and looking as if she could do with a bit of company. Say where, sir."

Hewson smiled. The man's chaff pleased him if only because, for the moment at least, it lent the unusual proceedings a much desired air of the commonplace.

"I'll place it myself, thanks," he said. "I'll find out where the drafts come from first."

"You won't find any down here. Well, good night, sir. I'm upstairs if you want me. Don't let 'em sneak up be'ind you and touch your neck with their cold and clammy 'ands. And you look out for that old Mrs. Dyer; I b'lieve she's taken a fancy to you."

Hewson laughed and wished the man good night. It was easier than he had expected. He wheeled the armchair—a heavy one upholstered in plush—a little way down the central gangway, and deliberately turned it so that its back was toward the effigy of Dr. Bourdette. For some undefined reason, he liked Dr. Bourdette a great deal less than his companions. Busying himself with arranging the chair, he was almost light-hearted, but when the attendant's footfalls had died away and a deep hush stole over the chamber, he realized that he had no slight ordeal before him.

The dim, unwavering light fell on the rows

of figures, which were so uncannily like human beings that the silence and the stillness seemed unnatural and even ghastly. He missed the sound of breathing, the rustling of clothes, the hundred and one minute noises one hears when even the deepest silence has fallen upon a crowd. But the air was as stagnant as water at the bottom of a standing pond. There was not a breath in the chamber to stir a curtain or rustle a hanging drapery or start a shadow. His own shadow, moving in response to a shifted arm or leg, was all that could be coaxed into motion. All was still to the gaze and silent to the ear. "It must be like this at the very bottom of the sea," he thought, wondering how to work the phrase into his story on the morrow.

He faced the sinister figures boldly enough. They were only waxworks. So long as he let that thought dominate all others, he promised himself that all would be well. It did not, however, save him long from the discomfort occasioned by the waxen stare of Dr. Bourdette, which, he knew, was directed upon him from behind. The eyes of the little Frenchman's effigy haunted and tormented him, and he itched with the desire to turn and look.

"Come!" he thought. "My nerves have started already. If I turn and look at that dressed up dummy, it will be an admission of funk."

45

And then another voice in his brain spoke to him.

"It's because you're afraid that you won't turn and look at him."

The two voices quarreled silently for a moment or two, and at last Hewson slewed his chair round a little and looked behind him.

Among the many figures standing in stiff, unnatural poses, the effigy of the dreadful little doctor stood out with a queer prominence, perhaps because a steady beam of light beat straight down upon it. Hewson flinched before the parody of mildness that some fiendishly skilled craftsman had managed to convey in wax, met the eyes for one agonized second, and turned again to face in the other direction.

"He's only a waxwork, like the rest of you," Hewson muttered defiantly. "You're all only waxworks."

They were only waxworks, yes, but waxworks don't move. Not that he had seen the slightest movement anywhere, but it struck him that, in the moment or two while he had looked behind him, there had been a subtle change in the grouping of the figures in front. Crippen, for instance, seemed to have turned at least one degree to the left. Or, thought Hewson, perhaps the illusion was due to the fact that he had not slewed his chair back into its exact original position. And there were Field and Grey, too; surely one of them had moved his hands. Hewson held his breath for a moment, and then drew his courage back to him as a man lifts a weight. He remembered the words of more than one news editor and laughed savagely to himself.

"And they tell me I've got no imagination!" he said beneath his breath.

He took a notebook from his pocket and wrote quickly.

"Mem.—Deathly silence and unearthly stillness of figures. Like being bottom of sea. Hypnotic eyes of Dr. Bourdette. Figures seem to move when not being watched."

He closed the book suddenly over his fingers and looked round quickly over his right shoulder. He had neither seen nor heard a movement, but it was as if some sixth sense had made him aware of one. He looked straight into the vapid countenance of Lefroy, which smiled vacantly back as if to say, "It wasn't I!"

Of course it wasn't he, or any of them; it was his own nerves. Or was it? Hadn't Crippen moved again during that moment when his attention was directed elsewhere? You couldn't trust that little man! Once you took your eyes off him, he took advantage of it to shift his position. That was what they were all doing, if he only knew it, he told himself, and he half rose out of his chair. This was not quite good enough! He was going. He wasn't going to spend the night with a lot of waxworks that moved while he wasn't looking.

Hewson sat down again. This was very cowardly and very absurd. They *were* only waxworks, and they *couldn't* move; let him hold that thought, and all would yet be well. Then why all that silent unrest about him—a subtle something in the air, which did not quite break the silence, and happened, whenever he looked, just beyond the boundaries of his vision?

He swung round quickly to encounter the mild but baleful stare of Dr. Bourdette. Then, without warning, he jerked his head back to stare straight at Crippen. Ha! He'd nearly caught Crippen that time! "You'd better be careful, Crippen—and all the rest of you! If I do see one of you move, I'll smash you to pieces! Do you hear?"

He ought to go, he told himself. Already he had experienced enough to write his story, or ten stories, for the matter of that. Well, then, why not go? The *Morning Echo* would be none the wiser as to how long he had stayed, nor would it care, so long as his story was a good one. Yes, but that night watchman upstairs would chaff him. And the manager—one never knew—perhaps the manager would quibble over that five-pound note that he needed so badly. He wondered if Rose were asleep or if she were lying awake and thinking of him. She'd laugh when he told her that he had imagined. . . .

This was a little too much! It was bad enough that the waxwork effigies of murderers should move when they weren't being watched, but it was intolerable that they should *breathe*. Somebody was breathing. Or was it his own breath that sounded to him as if it came from a distance? He sat rigid, listening and straining, until he exhaled with a long sigh. His own breath, after all, or, if not, something had divined that he was listening and had ceased breathing simultaneously with him.

Hewson jerked his head swiftly around and looked all about him out of haggard and haunted eyes. Everywhere his gaze encountered the vacant waxen faces, and everywhere he felt that, by just some least fraction of a second, he had missed seeing a movement of hand or foot, a silent opening or compression of lips, a flicker of eyelids, a look of human intelligence now smoothed out. They were like naughty children in a class, whispering, fidgeting, and laughing behind their teacher's back, but blandly innocent when his gaze was turned upon them.

This would not do! This distinctly would not do! He must clutch at something, grip with his mind upon something that belonged essentially to the workaday world, to the daylight London streets. He was Raymond Hewson, an unsuccessful journalist, a living and breathing man, and these figures grouped around him were only dummies, so they could neither move nor whisper. What did it matter if they were supposed to be lifelike effigies of murderers? They were only made of wax and sawdust, and they stood there for the entertainment of morbid sightseers. That was better! Now, what was that funny story that somebody had told him in the Falstaff yesterday?

He recalled part of it, but not all, for the gaze of Dr. Bourdette urged, challenged, and finally compelled him to turn.

Hewson half turned and then swung his chair so as to bring him face-to-face with the wearer of those dreadful hypnotic eyes. His own eyes were dilated, and his mouth, at first set in a grin of terror, lifted at the corners in a snarl. Then Hewson spoke and woke a hundred sinister echoes.

"You moved, blast you!" he cried. "Yes, you did, blast you! I saw you!"

Then he sat quite still, staring straight ahead, like a man found frozen in the Arctic snows.

Dr. Bourdette's movements were leisurely. He stepped off his pedestal with the mincing care of a lady alighting from a bus. The platform stood about two feet from the ground, and above the edge of it a plush-covered rope hung in arclike curves. Dr. Bourdette lifted up the rope until it formed an arch for him to pass under, stepped off the platform, and sat down on the edge, facing Hewson. Then he nodded and smiled and said, "Good evening.

"I need hardly tell you," he continued, in perfect English in which was traceable only the least foreign accent, "that not until I overheard the conversation between you and the worthy manager of this establishment did I suspect that I should have the pleasure of a companion here for the night. You cannot move or speak without my bidding, but you can hear me perfectly well. Something tells me that you are— shall I say nervous? My dear sir, have no illusions. I am not one of these contemptible effigies miraculously come to life. I am Dr. Bourdette himself."

He paused, coughed, and shifted his legs.

"Pardon me," he resumed, "but I am a little stiff. And let me explain. Circumstances with which I need not fatigue you have made it desirable that I should live in England. I was close to this building this evening when I saw a policeman regarding me a thought too curiously. I guessed that he intended to follow and perhaps ask me embarrassing questions, so I mingled with the crowd and came in here. An extra coin bought my admission to the chamber in which we now meet, and an inspiration showed me a certain means of escape.

"I raised a cry of fire, and when all the fools had rushed to the stairs, I stripped my effigy of the caped coat that you behold me wearing, donned it, hid my effigy under the platform at the back, and took its place on the pedestal.

"I own that I have since spent a very fatiguing evening, but fortunately I was not always being watched and had opportunities to draw an occasional deep breath and ease the rigidity of my pose. One small boy screamed and exclaimed that he saw me moving. I understood that he was to be whipped and put straight to bed on his return home, and I can only hope that the threat has indeed been executed to the letter.

"The manager's description of me, which I had the embarrassment of being compelled to overhear, was biased but not altogether inaccurate. Clearly I am not dead, although it is as well that the world thinks otherwise. His account of my hobby, which I have indulged for years, although, through necessity, less frequently of late, was in the main true, although not intelligently expressed. The world is divided between collectors and noncollectors. With the noncollectors we are not concerned. The collectors collect anything, according to their individual tastes, from money to cigarette cards, from moths to matchboxes. I collect throats."

He paused again and regarded Hewson's throat with mingled interest and disfavor.

"I am obliged to the chance that brought us together tonight," he continued, "and perhaps it would seem ungrateful to complain. From motives of personal safety, my activities have been somewhat curtailed of late years, and I am glad of this opportunity to gratify my somewhat unusual whim. But you have a skinny neck, sir, if you will overlook a personal remark. I should never have selected you from choice. I like men with thick necks . . . thick, red necks. . . ."

He fumbled in an inside pocket and took out something that he tested against a wet forefinger and then proceeded to pass gently to and fro across the palm of his left hand.

"This is a little French razor," he remarked blandly. "They are not much used in England, but perhaps you know them. One strops them on wood. The blade, you will observe, is very narrow. They do not cut very deep, but deep enough. In just one little moment you shall see for yourself. I shall ask you the little civil question of all the polite barbers: Does the razor suit you, sir?"

He rose up, a diminutive but menacing figure of evil, and approached Hewson with the silent, furtive step of a hunting panther.

"You will have the goodness," he said, "to raise your chin a little. Thank you, and a little more. Ah, thank you! *Merci, m'sieur....*"

Over one end of the chamber was a thick skylight of frosted glass that, by day, let in a few sickly and filtered rays from the floor above. After sunrise these began to mingle with the subdued light from the electric bulbs, and this mingled illumination added a certain ghastliness to a scene that needed no additional touch of horror.

The waxwork figures stood apathetically in their places, waiting to be admired or execrated by the crowds who would presently wander fearfully among them. In their midst, in the center gangway, Hewson sat still, leaning far back in his armchair. His chin was uptilted, as if he were waiting to receive attention from a barber, and, although there was not a scratch upon his throat or anywhere upon his body, he was cold and dead. His previous employers were wrong in having credited him with no powers of imagination.

Dr. Bourdette, on his pedestal, watched the dead man unemotionally. He did not move, nor was he capable of motion. But then, after all, he was only a waxwork.

H. R. WAKEFIELD

Used Car

Mr. Arthur Canning, senior partner in the prosperous firm of solicitors that bore his name, was convinced—for the purposes of family debate—that he neither required nor could afford another car. But his daughter Angela, aged nineteen, derided the former objection, while his wife, Joan, pooh-poohed the second. A shabby five-year-old that couldn't do fifty with a tail wind outraged Angela's sense of social decency, and her mother knew all about how good business had been lately. So their sire and husband, like a good democrat, bowed to the will of the majority and took a walk one afternoon down Great Portland Street, where are rehearsed the fables of the car-changers and where are situated the seats of those who sell pups. No new car for him, if he could get what he wanted secondhand.

Presently he halted outside a shop and began to examine, with apparent interest, an impressive saloon that was thrusting its comely bonnet to the edge of the pavement and that announced, by a card slung from its radiator cap, that it was a Highway Straight Eight and a superb bargain at £350. This was in the halcyon mid-twenties, before the investing public had been initiated into the arcana of high finance through the agency of juries, coroners' and otherwise, and could still contemplate a box of matches without bursting into tears. In those days one could not buy a magnificent used car for five pounds down and a few small weekly installments; so the Highway *did* look like good value to Mr. Canning.

A trim and sprightly young salesman came out from the interior and wished Mr. Canning a good afternoon.

"I'm rather interested in this Highway," said the latter. "I frequently drove in one in America, but I can't seem to remember ever seeing one here."

The young man had been discreetly diagnosing Mr. Canning's shrewd and determined countenance and had already decided that he was a foeman worthy of his steel. (Sometimes it was merely a pleasure to serve a customer!) But this person was clearly not one whom he could easily persuade that £350 was an irreducible minimum. "No, sir," he replied. "They're very fine cars, but their output is small, and they're too expensive for the British market."

"How did this one come into your hands?"

"An American gentleman brought it over with him and disposed of it to us. It's a 1924 model and a *marvelous* bargain."

"Of course, that remains to be seen," replied Mr. Canning, with a sophisticated smile and in the tone of one who had enjoyed, more or less, a higher automobile education. Whereupon he made a thorough superficial examination of the car and then made up his mind.

"I shall want it vetted by my expert," he said, "and if his verdict is favorable, I will make you an offer."

"I'm afraid—" began the young man.

"Here's his address," continued Mr. Canning imperturbably. "Deliver it there tomorrow, and I'll let him know it's coming. Good afternoon."

In the course of the next few days, Mrs. and Miss Canning inspected the Highway and pronounced a qualified approval of its appearance and appointments, and the expert gave its mechanical doings an A1 certificate, with the result that a check for £270 changed hands, and Tonks, Mr. Canning's chauffeur, drove it down to Grey Lodge, near Guildford, Surrey. The expert drew Mr. Canning's attention to a rather large dark stain on the fawn corduroy behind the back seat, saying that he hoped none of his men were responsible. Mr. Canning reassured him by declaring that it had been there all the time. He had noticed it in the shop, he said.

Mr. Canning, on attaining a certain affluence, had built himself a very comfortable and aesthetically satisfying house in West Surrey. Like everything else about him and his, it suggested supertax but not death duties. His social standing was well established in the neighborhood, for Mrs. Canning, a handsome, well-upholstered matron, had a shrewd Scottish flair for entertainment and a flexible faculty for making the right people feel at home; and Angela was lively and decorative and hit balls about with superior skill. On reaching home the next evening, he found these ladies had already taken a trip in the car. Their verdict was favorable. Mrs. Canning liked the springing and the back seat, though one of the windows rattled, while Angela was satisfied it would do seventy. "But," she added, "Jumbo loathes it."

"How do you mean?" asked her father.

"Oh, all the time we were out he was whining and fussing, and when we got home, he dashed out into the garden with his tail between his legs."

"Well, he'll have to get used to it," said Mr. Canning, in a firm tone which implied that he would stand no nonsense from that pampered and good-for-nothing liver spaniel. "Has Tonks got that stain off the cloth?"

"He's working at it this evening," replied Angela. "It only wants rubbing with petrol."

After dinner, while they were sitting round the fire in the drawing room, Jumbo with his paws in the grate, Mr. Canning tried an experiment by giving his celebrated imitation of a motor horn, which usually aroused anticipatory ecstasies in Jumbo. This time, however, he stared up uncertainly at his master, and the motions of his tail suggested no more than mere politeness. "You see," said Angela, who possessed a deep insight into the animal, "he doesn't know whether you mean the old car or the new."

"Oh, rot!" said her father. "He's sleepy." But he was half convinced. "Anyhow," he presently continued, "I'll take him with me to South Hill on Saturday. I've always said he was a perfect half-wit."

"He's a perfect *darling!*" said Mrs. Canning indignantly. "Come here, my sweet." Jumbo lurched reluctantly over to her, his demeanor suggesting that, while affectionate appreciation of his charms was gratifying, when a fellow was sleeping peacefully with his paws in the grate, it was a bit thick to keep on disturbing him. "We're going over to the Talbots' tomorrow," Mrs. Canning went on, "but we'll be back in time to send the car to the station if it's raining." Her husband grunted drowsily and returned to his perusal of *Country Life.*

"Hullo, William," said Angela at three o'clock the next afternoon. "I see you haven't done anything about that stain."

The chauffeur appeared somewhat piqued at this insinuation, his manner implying that, considering he had taught Miss Angela to drive when her hair was still in a pigtail, she ought to treat him with more deference. "I did my best, Miss," he replied. "I gave it a stiff rubbing with petrol, but it didn't make no difference."

"I wonder what it is," said Angela.

"I don't know, Miss, but last night it felt sticky to the touch."

"It's quite dry now," she declared. "Have another go at it this evening. Ah, here's mother."

The Talbots lived some twenty miles away. Miss Talbot had been at school with Angela. Bob Talbot had lately taken to blushing heavily when her name was mentioned, much to his chagrin and the delight of the local covey of flappers. The Talbots were nice people, well connected, best-quality-county, and rather hard up. The Cannings were nice people, only just emerging from the professional-urban chrysalis, and on the financial upgrade. So the two families were at once contrasted and complementary. They enjoyed each other's company, so it was after six when the Cannings started for home in the much admired Highway. After they had covered a short distance, Angela said, "Rather a frowst, Mother. Shall I open a window?"

"Yes, do, dear. Have you noticed a queer smell, musty and sickly?"

"Yes, it's just frowst," replied Angela. "I'll open the one on your side. The wind's blowing hard on mine." She leaned and then said sharply, "Don't, Mother. Why did you do that?"

"Do what, dear?"

"Put your hand on my throat?"

"What *are* you talking about? I never did anything of the sort!"

Angela let the window down and then was silent. Why had Mama told that silly lie? She'd caught her throat quite hard. It had almost hurt. It wasn't a bit like her, either, to do such an idiotic thing or to pretend that she hadn't. Oh, well, everyone was a silly ass at times; she'd think about something else. She'd think about that old mutt, Bob; he really had been rather sweet. "Mrs. Robert Talbot"—how did that sound? Not too bad, but she didn't want to be Mrs. anybody yet awhile. She mustn't let him get too fond of her till she was sure; but she mustn't choke him off too much. How this judicious *via media* was to be followed was by no means clear to her, but the feat of having settled the principle of the thing so soothed her and restored her temper that she now regarded her parent's infelicitous pleasantry with tolerance. When she was getting out of the car, she touched the back of it to steady herself. Before following her mother into the house, she turned to Tonks, prinking her fingers together.

"That stain's damp," she said to him.

Tonks switched on the light and felt it for himself. "P'raps it is a bit, Miss," he said doubtfully. "I'll work on it again tonight."

In the hall Angela examined her fingers closely. Then she rubbed them with her handkerchief and scrutinized that. She wrinkled her nose, as if puzzled, and went up to her room.

The next morning, Saturday, was brilliantly fine, so Mr. Canning ordered the car to be round at nine-thirty. He was awaiting it, with Jumbo by his side, when it entered the drive from the garage turning. Jumbo gave it one searching glance and was off at a gallop for the garden. "Jumbo, Jumbo, come here!" cried his master imperiously. There was no response, so Mr. Canning, a gleam in his eye, set off in pursuit. There he was, the old devil, peeping round from behind the silver birch. A fruitless and temper-rousing chase ensued, but Jumbo, though obviously alarmed and despondent, was neither to be cajoled nor trapped, so Mr. Canning, after reviling him copiously from a distance and promising him prolonged corporal punishment in the near future, went back to the car. He was ruffled, and the sight of that stain irritated him still more. "Can't you get it out, William?" he asked sharply.

The chauffeur had reasons of his own for disliking the subject and replied respectfully, but firmly, that he'd done his best but could make no impression on it.

"Humph," said Mr. Canning. "South Hill," and lit a cigar.

He defeated his ancient rival, Bob Pelham, in both rounds, lunched well, perspired satisfactorily, and had a large whisky and soda just before leaving for home. So he was feeling full of good cheer but inclined for repose when he came out of the clubhouse to drive home. He noticed Pelham emerge from the locker room, go to the car, and look in at the window. A moment later he was by his side. "Hello, *there* you are," said Pelham. "Funny thing—I could have sworn I saw you inside."

"Then you had better not have another drink," said Canning.

"Must be that," replied the other. "All the

same, I could have sworn it. Well, safe home, and ten-thirty today week, if it's a decent day. I'll have cured that blasted hook by then, so don't forget your wallet."

"If you prefer to slice, that's your business," replied Mr. Canning. "So long. I think I'll sit with you, William," he continued. "It smells stuffy inside there."

It was too dark to see more than was disclosed in the headlight's beam, so he soon closed his eyes. And then of a sudden it seemed to him that the speed of the car increased violently. He opened his eyes with the intention of speaking to Tonks and found he couldn't move, nor could he speak, and there was something pressing hard into his back. What was the matter? What had happened? Where were they? This wasn't the Guildford road! They were tearing madly across a plain, a region dim and hazy, and as they flashed past a crossroads, there was a signpost of strange shape, on which he thought he could just read the letters CHICA. And then he heard a vile whisper just behind him: "Let 'em have it." For a moment he knew the unique, agonized terror of certain and imminent death.

There was a scream, a flame through his head, a crash—and Tonks was saying, in a very startled voice, "What's the matter, sir? What's the matter? Have you cut yourself?"

The car pulled up hard on its brakes. For a moment Mr. Canning sat trembling and silent, then he said hoarsely, "What has happened?"

"You've put your elbow bang through the glass, sir. Let me look. It's all right, sir. You're not cut."

"What was that scream?" asked Mr. Canning, vaguely examining the elbow of his coat.

"Scream, sir?"

"Yes, a woman's scream."

"I 'eard no scream, sir."

"It's all right," said Mr. Canning after a pause. "I went to sleep and must have had a dream. Drive on, but go slowly. Get a new glass put in on Monday." As he got out of the car half an hour later, he said, "I'll explain to the ladies."

"Very good, sir," replied Tonks. "Are you feeling all right, sir?"

"Quite, quite."

Jumbo was peering round the banisters on the first landing, his eyes rolling with apprehension. "Hullo, Jumbo," said his master. "Good boy!" Jumbo's ears soared in sheer astonishment and relief and he lumbered hurriedly down the stairs to consolidate this unexpected armistice. Mr. Canning twisted his ears and smacked his rump. "You deserve a good hiding, you old rascal, but I think I'll let you off this time."

At dinner he alluded, with rather elaborate

casualness, to his encounter with the glass. "What a funny position to get your elbow into," commented his wife.

"Oh, I don't know," he replied. "I was asleep, and it was jerked up, I suppose."

"Has Tonks got that stain out?" she asked.

"Oh, confound that stain!" said Angela brusquely. "I'm fed up with it, and anyhow, it doesn't show much."

"Yes, I think we'll leave it for the present," agreed Mr. Canning. "The stuff, whatever it is, seems to have soaked right into the cloth." He felt he didn't want to hear another word about that car for the time being.

Later, as he lay in bed waiting for sleep, he was uneasily wondering if he were going to experience another beastly dream like the one in the car. Of course it had been a dream, though he'd never had one like it before. That scream! He could still hear it in a fading, echoed way, a cry of agony and terror. And that filthy whisper! He shivered a little. Oh, well, it was simply that he wasn't used to dreaming so vividly. That was all. He began to play over again in his head his first round. First hole: good drive, fair brassie to the left of the green, nice pitch over the bunker, and a couple of putts. One up. Second hole: rather a sliced tee shot, a slightly topped number three iron, and then—and then it was eight o'clock on Sunday morning, and Jumbo was scratching on the door for entry and a biscuit, the just reward of a blameless, though often misjudged, dog.

During the next few days, neither the ladies nor Mr. Canning had occasion to use the car after dark. Mrs. Canning developed a relaxed throat, and cheery, chatty Dr. Gables came to have a look at it. "Like to see the new car?" asked Angela as the doctor was preparing to take his leave.

"All right," said the doctor. "If only we'd had a decent flu winter, I'd have invested in another one myself."

"Cheer up," replied Angela. "The mumps and measles season may be better. You go on. I'll get the garage key and catch up." As she came out of the front door, she saw the doctor disappearing round the turning to the garage.

A moment later she was mildly surprised to hear him saying, "Hullo, good evening." When she caught up, he asked, in a rather puzzled tone, "What's the matter with Tonks?"

"Tonks?" said Angela. "He's gone home ages ago."

"No, he hasn't. I saw him standing at the garage door, but when I spoke to him, he disappeared round the corner. Rude fellow!"

"I don't think it could have been he," said

Angela rather shortly. She unlocked the door and switched on the light, and they went in.

"Nice-looking bus," remarked the doctor. "Never seen a Highway before; looks like a very neat job." He lifted the bonnet flap and gazed knowingly at its digestive system. "Let's see the inside." He opened the door, peered in, and then sniffed once or twice. He climbed in, sat down, and put his head back. "Hullo," he exclaimed, "my head's sticking to something!" He turned round and saw the stain. "It was sticking to that. What is it?"

"Oh, I don't know," said Angela. "It was there when we got the car. Seen enough?"

"Yes," replied the doctor, getting out. "Nice bus. And now I must be off. I've got to assist in increasing the population in an hour—in these times a thoroughly antisocial act—but a man must live. Ring me in the morning and tell me how your mother is. Make her keep on at that gargle. Good night, my dear."

As he strolled home, he was thinking to himself, "That car has a very odd reek. When I smelled it, I could almost believe I was back at the dressing station near Bois Grenier. Perhaps that's why I took a mild dislike to the car. I suppose that chap Tonks is okay. Always thought he was a very steady fellow, yet it was queer the way he slipped off just now. Of course it *might* have been someone else. None of my business, anyway."

Saturday morning turned out to be chilly and boisterous, with a falling barometer and an unmistakable smell of coming rain, so Mr. Pelham, who had drunk more port than he'd realized at a Masonic dinner the night before and had greeted the dawn with loathing, quite agreed with Mr. Canning that it was no day for golf. The latter took a stroll round his domain after breakfast. Eventually he turned into the garage. Tonks was cleaning the car. Mr. Canning greeted him and asked him how he was. "Quite well, thank you, sir," he replied. However, his looks and the tone of his voice somewhat belied him.

"Hullo," thought Mr. Canning, "something wrong." Tonks was a cockney, and so was his master; they belonged, by origin, to much the same class. They, therefore, had an instinctive understanding of each other. Between Mr. Canning and rustics of all social strata there was a great gulf of misunderstanding, but he knew his Londoner of the Tonks type like the back of his hand, and there was something on his mind.

"Now then, William," he said gently but firmly, "what's the matter?"

"Nothing, sir."

"You've been with me seven years and six months."

"Yes, sir," he replied, rather gratified at this accuracy.

"And how many lies have you told me in that time?"

"None, deliberate, sir."

"Then don't begin now, William. What is it—money, a woman, some such trouble?"

"None of 'em, sir."

"I didn't expect so. Then what is it?"

"It sounds like foolishness, sir."

"Leave me to judge that."

"Well, sir, I get a bit scared."

"Scared, scared! In what way?" asked Mr. Canning, wondering vaguely why he'd somehow expected some such answer.

"That's what I'm not sure about," replied Tonks, his confidence released now that the ice was broken. "That's why it sounds like foolishness, but it seemed to begin like just as soon as the Highway came in."

"Came into the garage, d'you mean?"

"Yes, sir."

"Well, what happened?"

"At first it was just that I had a feeling of someone about, someone watching me. I looked around but couldn't exactly see no one. But somehow it seemed to me there was three of 'em. And it's been like that since, sir. It's always after dark. And I've felt they was coming along be'ind me and then standing and watching.''

"Is that all?" asked Mr. Canning after a pause.

"Well, sir, one evening when I was putting 'er away—I'd just opened the door and was about to switch on the light—it seemed to me there was whispering going on just by me, and I thought someone touched me. And there've been other things, other goings-on, as it were, whenever I've been 'ere after dark. I never feels alone, sir, always expecting something. Now, I 'ad an aunt, sir, who saw things and 'eard things that wasn't really there, and she went out of 'er mind later on, and I've got the wind up that I'm going the same way. I was thinking p'raps I oughtn't to drive, if I was going that way.''

"Nonsense!" replied Mr. Canning sharply. "Nothing of the kind. You're as sane as anyone else.''

"I certainly feels it, sir, but then, why do I think I sees and 'ears and feels things?''

"It's nothing, nothing! Many people have that sort of experience.''

"Do they really, sir?''

"Yes! Yes! Think no more about it.''

"All right, I'll try, sir.''

For the next hour Mr. Canning walked round

and round the garden. An ugly, insinuating notion was knocking for admittance to his mind. Something at which he'd always scoffed; something the possibility of which he'd always eagerly derided. For a moment the echo of a scream rang in his head, and the memory of a look on Angela's face came back to him. Of course it was all ridiculous. Silly fancies! He'd shake his mind of them. It was a depressing day, and he'd done a very hard week's work. It was all tommyrot! He began to whistle a cheerful little tune and went indoors for a glass of that most excellent new sherry.

On Thursday Angela drove over to a neighbor's house to play tennis on their hard court. When she got home again, Walker, the butler, who let her in, noticed that she was looking tired and upset. She told him rather brusquely to get her some brandy. She swallowed it at a gulp, and her color began to return. During dinner she was silent and preoccupied. Her father noticed it and suggested she might have caught her mother's cold. She answered irritably that she was perfectly all right; but he observed, also, that she drank more wine than was her wont and that her nerves had got somewhat the better of her. After dinner she pretended to read but went early to bed.

By Monday morning Mrs. Canning's throat

was better, but Dr. Gables refused to allow her out of doors. She was a busy, active person who resented any kind of restraint. What made it worse was that Angela had gone up to Town to shop. She felt lonely and bored. Household chores occupied the morning more or less. After lunch she slept a little, did her nails, and tried to concentrate on a novel, which its publisher adroitly insinuated had almost been banned. But she found that its author, a young woman of twenty, had really very little to teach a wife and mother of forty-nine. Sex, she thought with a yawn, was nearly always just the same, however much one stupidly hoped it was going to be different. After tea she felt something had to be done. Her temper was going; Angela oughtn't to have left her; Jumbo's snores got on her nerves; she wanted to scream. Dr. Gables was just an old fusser. Suddenly she made up her mind, rang the bell, and told Martha to tell William she wanted the car round at once. She soothed her conscience by wrapping herself up in many garments and went downstairs.

"Just drive around for an hour or so," she told Tonks, "and keep off the main roads."

For a time she gave herself up to the delight of being on the move again and thinking how lovely the county of Surrey looked in the last rays of the sinking sun. Then she began considering this and that rather lazily. It was very warm in the car. Her thoughts became even less coherent, and presently her head nodded. Sometime later she woke up with a start, under the vague impression that someone had touched her. It was quite dark, she noticed. Weren't they going very fast? What was the matter with her? She opened and closed her eyes very quickly several times. Then, very stealthily, she tried to move her elbows. She must keep quite calm and think. She had gone out for a drive with William and must have gone to sleep. Why was William wearing that funny cap? And who was that on the seat beside him? And why couldn't she move her elbows? It was just as if they were gripped by two hands. What had happened? Had she gone mad? Suddenly she lunged forward convulsively, and it seemed to her that she was wrenched back and a hand went fiercely to her throat. She twisted, writhed, and tried to scream. There were flashes of flame before her bursting eyes, and, as her head was forced agonizingly back, she felt life choked from her.

She was lying on a grass bank beside the road. Tonks was bending over her and trying to force something in a glass between her lips. Someone else was supporting her head. "Is she subject to fits?" asked the latter.

"No, sir. I don't think this is a fit. She's coming to."

Mrs. Canning's eyes opened, and her hands went to her throat. "Where are they? Who's that?" she screamed.

"It's all right, madam," said Tonks gently. "You fainted." Her head fell back again and her eyes closed.

"We'd better take her into the house," said the stranger.

"It's very good of you, sir," said Tonks, "but I'd rather get her home."

"As you say," replied the other. The two men carried her into the car.

"Would you mind driving, sir?" said Tonks. "I think I'd better be inside with her. It's the first turning on the left about two miles along."

"She's better," said Dr. Gables, two hours later, "but she's had a very severe shock of some kind. She seems to imagine she was attacked in the car—not quite herself mentally yet. I've given her a strong sedative, and the nurse knows what to do. I'll be along first thing in the morning."

"Father," said Angela, when the doctor had gone, "there's something vile about that car!" She was very white and still trembling. "I know it! I know it! I didn't say anything about it at the time, but on Thursday when I was driving home, it got dark just before we entered the drive, and I suddenly felt someone beside me. It was only for a moment—till I saw the lights of the house—but there *was* someone there."

Mr. Canning stared past her for a time before replying. Then he said, "It shall not be used again."

The next day he made inquiries, first at the car shop in Great Portland Street and then at the American Express Company, with the result that he sent the following letter to an address in Chicago:

Dear Sir,
I understand that you were the previous owner of a Highway car that I recently purchased. It is not easy to put into words what I have to say, but, as the result of certain experiences that I and members of my household have had with this car, I have decided to dispose of it in some way. At the same time I feel a certain strong reluctance about allowing others to suffer the same experiences, which might happen if I sold it. All this may be incomprehensible to you; if so, please do not trouble to reply. If, however, you can throw any light on the matter, it might be very useful as a guide to me.
Yours faithfully,
A. T. Canning

Three weeks later he received the following reply:

SHUDDERS

—— Michigan Avenue,
Chicago, Ill.

Dear Mr. Canning,

In one way I was very glad to get your letter; in another it made me feel terribly bad. I knew when I did it, and I've known ever since, that I'd no business to turn in that Highway. It was just a case of feeling one way and acting another. Now, I can't figure out just what's wrong with that car, but I *do* know I wouldn't take another night ride in it for a thousand bucks. That's why I was dead wrong to turn it in, and I've no alibi. Here's its record. There was a well-known moll in this city, named Blond Beulah Kratz, who was in with a bunch of tough gangsters—she covered the blackmail and vice angle. She had a temporary boyfriend, a thirty-minute egg, named Snowbird Sordone. And they figured it that they ought to have collected more of the loot from some job. So they tried to double-cross the rest of the gang. Well, they were taken for a trip in the country one night, and their bodies were found in that Highway next day —it ran out of gas, I guess. The blond was knifed and strangled—that gang took no chances—and Snowbird had some big slugs through his back. Well, our district attorney, a friend of mine, took over the car and then pretty soon didn't feel so crazy about it and passed it on to me, just when I was coming to Europe, so I took it with me. Well, after I'd had a few rides in it, I turned it in quick, just like that, and I guess you know why.

Now, Mr. Canning, what I want you to do is this. First of all, forgive me for letting you in for an unpleasant experience. And then just fill in the enclosed check for the amount you paid for the Highway. Then I want you to take that automobile and tip it into the ocean or stall it on a level crossing or match it with Carnera. Anyway, do something to it so that no one will ride in it again and get so scared the way I did and, I guess, you did. I forgot to say that the birds who bumped the blond and the Snowbird got the electric chair here.

If I get to Europe again, I'll look you up, if I may. Now, please, Mr. Canning, fill in that check right away, and then I'll know you've forgiven me, and I'll feel better.

Yours truly,

George A. Camshott

Mr. Canning, with a clear conscience, subsequently carried out all these instructions.

H. G. WELLS

The Inexperienced Ghost

The scene amidst which Clayton told his last story comes back very vividly to my mind. There he sat, for the greater part of the time, in the corner of the authentic settle by the spacious open fire, and Sanderson sat beside him smoking the Broseley clay that bore his name. There was Evans, and that marvel among actors, Wish, who is also a modest man. We had all come down to the Mermaid Club that Saturday morning, except Clayton, who had slept there overnight—which, indeed, gave him the opening of his story. We had golf until golfing was invisible; we had dined, and we were in that mood of tranquil kindliness when men will suffer a story. When Clayton began to tell one, we naturally supposed he was lying. It may be that indeed he was lying—of that the reader will speedily be able to judge as well as I. He began, it is true, with an air of matter-of-fact anecdote, but that, we thought, was only the incurable artifice of the man.

"I say!" he remarked, after a long consideration of the upward rain of sparks from the log that Sanderson had thumped. "You know I was alone here last night?"

"Except for the domestics," said Wish.

"Who sleep in the other wing," said Clayton. "Yes. Well—" He pulled at his cigar for some little time, as though he still hesitated about his confidence. Then he said, quite quietly, "I caught a ghost!"

"Caught a ghost, did you?" said Sanderson. "Where is it?"

And Evans, who admires Clayton immensely and has been four weeks in America, shouted, "*Caught* a ghost, did you, Clayton? I'm glad of it! Tell us all about it right now."

Clayton said he would in a minute and asked him to shut the door.

He looked apologetically at me. "There's no eavesdropping, of course, but we don't want to upset our very excellent service with any rumors of ghosts in the place. There's too much shadow and oak paneling to trifle with that. And this, you know, wasn't a regular ghost. I don't think it will come again—ever."

"You mean to say you didn't keep it?" said Sanderson.

"I hadn't the heart to," said Clayton.

And Sanderson said he was surprised.

We laughed, and Clayton looked aggrieved. "I know," he said, with the flicker of a smile, "but the fact is it really *was* a ghost, and I'm as sure of it as I am that I am talking to you now. I'm not joking. I mean what I say."

Sanderson drew deeply at his pipe, with one reddish eye on Clayton, and then emitted a thin jet of smoke, which was more eloquent than many words.

Clayton chose to ignore this. "It is the strangest thing that has ever happened in my life. You know I never believed in ghosts or anything of the sort before, ever; and then, you know, I bag one in a corner, and the whole business is in my hands."

He meditated still more profoundly, and produced and began to pierce a second cigar with a curious little stabber he affected.

"You talked to it?" asked Wish.

"For the space, probably, of an hour."

"Chatty?" I said, joining the party of the skeptics.

"The poor devil was in trouble," said Clayton, bowed over his cigar end and with the very faintest note of reproof.

"Sobbing?" someone asked.

Clayton heaved a realistic sigh at the memory. "Good Lord," he said, "yes!" And then, "Poor fellow! Yes."

"Where did you strike it?" asked Evans, in his best American accent.

"I never realized," said Clayton, ignoring him, "the poor sort of thing a ghost might be." And he hung us up again for a time, while he sought for matches in his pocket and lit his cigar.

"I took an advantage," he reflected at last.

We were none of us in a hurry. "A character," he said, "remains just the same character, for all that it's been disembodied. That's a thing we too often forget. People with a certain strength or fixity of purpose may have ghosts of a certain strength and fixity of purpose—most haunting ghosts, you know, must be as one-idea'd as monomaniacs and as obstinate as mules to come back again and again. This poor creature wasn't." He suddenly looked up rather queerly, and his eye went round the room. "I say it," he said, "in all kindliness, but that is the plain truth of the case. Even at the first glance he struck me as weak."

He punctuated with the help of his cigar.

"I came upon him, you know, in the long passage. His back was toward me, and I saw him first. Right off I knew him for a ghost. He was transparent and whitish; clean through his chest I could see the glimmer of the little window at the end. And not only his physique but also his attitude struck me as being weak. He

83

looked, you know, as though he didn't know in the slightest whatever he meant to do. One hand was on the paneling and the other fluttered to his mouth. Like—*so!*"

"What sort of physique?" said Sanderson.

"Lean. You know that sort of young man's neck that has two great flutings down the back, here and here—so! And a little meanish head with scrubby hair and rather bad ears. Shoulders bad, narrower than the hips; turndown collar, ready-made short jacket, trousers baggy and a little frayed at the heels. That's how he took me. I came very quietly up the staircase. I did not carry a light, you know—the candles are on the landing table and there is that lamp—and I was in my list slippers, and I saw him as I came up. I stopped dead at that—taking him in. I wasn't a bit afraid. I think that in most of these affairs one is never nearly so afraid or excited as one imagines one would be. I was surprised and interested. I thought, 'Good Lord! Here's a ghost at last! And I haven't believed in ghosts during the last five-and-twenty years.'"

"Um," said Wish.

"I suppose I wasn't on the landing a moment before he found out I was there. He turned on me sharply, and I saw the face of an immature young man, a weak nose, a scrubby little mustache, a feeble chin. So for an instant we stood

—he looking over his shoulder at me—and regarded one another. Then he seemed to remember his high calling. He turned round, drew himself up, projected his face, raised his arms, spread his hands in approved ghost fashion—came toward me. As he did so his little jaw dropped, and he emitted a faint, drawn-out 'Boo.' No, it wasn't—not a bit dreadful. I'd dined. I'd had a bottle of champagne, and, being all alone, perhaps two or three—perhaps even four or five—whiskies, so I was as solid as rocks and no more frightened than if I'd been assailed by a frog. 'Boo!' I said. 'Nonsense. You don't belong to *this* place. What are you doing here?'

"I could see him wince. 'Boo—oo,' he said.

"'Boo—be hanged! Are you a member?' I said; and just to show I didn't care a pin for him, I stepped through a corner of him and made to light my candle. 'Are you a member?' I repeated, looking at him sideways.

"He moved a little so as to stand clear of me, and his bearing became crestfallen. 'No,' he said, in answer to the persistent interrogation of my eye. 'I'm not a member—I'm a ghost.'

"'Well, that doesn't give you the run of the Mermaid Club. Is there anyone you want to see, or anything of that sort?' And doing it as steadily as possible for fear that he should mistake the carelessness of whisky for the distraction of fear, I got my candle alight. I turned on him, holding it. 'What are you doing here?' I asked once more.

"He had dropped his hands and stopped his booing, and there he stood, abashed and awkward, the ghost of a weak, silly, aimless young man. 'I'm haunting,' he said.

"'You haven't any business to,' I said in a quiet voice.

"'I'm a ghost,' he said, as if in defense.

"'That may be, but you haven't any business to haunt here. This is a respectable private club; people often stop here with nursemaids and children, and, with you going about in the careless way you do, some poor little mite could easily come upon you and be scared out of her wits. I suppose you didn't think of that.'

"'No, sir,' he said, 'I didn't.'

"'You should have done. You haven't any claim on the place, have you? Weren't murdered here, or anything of that sort?'

"'None, sir; but I thought as it was old and oak-paneled—'

"'That's *no* excuse.' I regarded him firmly. 'Your coming here is a mistake,' I said, in a tone of friendly superiority. I feigned to see if I had my matches, and then looked up at him frankly. 'If I were you, I wouldn't wait for cockcrow—I'd vanish right away.'

"He looked embarrassed. 'The fact *is,* sir—' he began.

"'I'd vanish,' I said, driving it home.

"'The fact is, sir, that—somehow—I can't.'

"'You *can't?*'

"'No, sir. There's something I've forgotten. I've been hanging about here since midnight last night, hiding in the cupboards of the empty bedrooms and things like that. I'm flurried. I've never come haunting before, and it seems to put me out.'

"'Put you out?'

"'Yes, sir. I've tried to do it several times, and it doesn't come off. There's some little thing has slipped me, and I can't get back.'

"That, you know, rather bowled me over. He looked at me in such an abject way that for the life of me I couldn't keep up quite the high hectoring vein I had adopted. 'That's queer,' I said, and as I spoke I fancied I heard someone moving about down below. 'Come into my room and tell me more about it,' I said. I didn't, of course, understand this, and I tried to take him by the arm. But, of course, you might as well have tried to take hold of a puff of smoke! I had forgotten my number, I think; anyhow, I remember going into several bedrooms—it was lucky I was the only soul in that wing—until I saw my traps. 'Here we are,' I said, and sat down in

87

the armchair. 'Sit down and tell me all about it. It seems to me you have got yourself into a jolly awkward position, old chap.'

"Well, he said he wouldn't sit down; he'd prefer to flit up and down the room, if it was all the same to me. And so he did, and in a little while we were deep in a long and serious talk. And presently, you know, something of those whiskies and sodas evaporated out of me, and I began to realize just a little what a thundering rum and weird business it was that I was in. There he was, semitransparent—the proper conventional phantom, and noiseless except for his ghost of a voice—flitting to and fro in that nice, clean, chintz-hung old bedroom. You could see the gleam of the copper candlesticks through him, and the lights on the brass fender, and the corners of the framed engravings on the wall, and there he was telling me all about this wretched little life of his that had recently ended on earth. He hadn't a particularly honest face, you know, but being transparent, of course, he couldn't avoid telling the truth."

"Eh?" said Wish, suddenly sitting up in his chair.

"What?" said Clayton.

"Being transparent—couldn't avoid telling the truth—I don't see it," said Wish.

"*I* don't see it," said Clayton, with inimitable

assurance. "But it *is* so, I can assure you, nevertheless. I don't believe he got once a nail's breadth off the Bible truth. He told me how he had been killed—he went down into a London basement with a candle to look for a leakage of gas—and described himself as a senior English master in a London private school when that release occurred."

"Poor wretch!" said I.

"That's what I thought, and the more he talked the more I thought it. There he was, purposeless in life and purposeless out of it. He talked of his father and mother and his schoolmaster, and all who had ever been anything to him in the world, meanly. He had been too sensitive, too nervous; none of them had ever valued him properly or understood him, he said. He had never had a real friend in the world, I think; he had never had a success. He had shirked games and failed examinations. 'It's like that with some people,' he said. 'Whenever I got into the examination room or anywhere, everything seemed to go.' Engaged to be married, of course—to another oversensitive person, I suppose—when the indiscretion with the gas escape ended his affairs.

"'And where are you now?' I asked. 'Not in. . . .'

"He wasn't clear on that point at all. The

impression he gave was of a sort of vague, intermediate state, a special reserve for souls too nonexistent for anything so positive as either sin or virtue. *I* don't know. He was much too egotistical and unobservant to give me any clear idea of the kind of place, kind of country, there is on the Other Side of Things. Wherever he was, he seems to have fallen in with a set of kindred spirits: ghosts of weak Cockney young men, who were on a footing of Christian names, and among these there was certainly a lot of talk about 'going haunting' and things like that. Yes—going haunting! They seemed to think 'haunting' a tremendous adventure, and most of them funked it all the time. And so primed, you know, he had come."

"But really!" said Wish to the fire.

"These are the impressions he gave me, anyhow," said Clayton modestly. "I may, of course, have been in a rather uncritical state, but that was the sort of background he gave to himself. He kept flitting up and down, with his thin voice going—talking, talking about his wretched self, and never a word of clear, firm statement from first to last. He was thinner and sillier and more pointless than if he had been real and alive. Only then, you know, he would not have been in my bedroom here—if he *had* been alive. I should have kicked him out."

"Of course," said Evans, "there *are* poor mortals like that."

"And there's just as much chance of their having ghosts as the rest of us," I admitted.

"What gave a sort of point to him, you know, was the fact that he did seem within limits to have found himself out. The mess he had made of haunting had depressed him terribly. He had been told it would be a 'lark'; he had come expecting it to be a 'lark,' and here it was, nothing but another failure added to his record! He proclaimed himself an utter out-and-out failure. He said, and I can quite believe it, that he had never tried to do anything all his life that he hadn't made a perfect mess of—and through all the wastes of eternity he never would. If he had had sympathy, perhaps— He paused at that and stood regarding me. He remarked that, strange as it might seem to me, nobody, not anyone, ever, had given him the amount of sympathy I was giving him now. I could see what he wanted straightaway, and I determined to head him off at once. I may be a brute, you know, but being the Only Real Friend, the recipient of the confidences of one of these egotistical weaklings, ghost or body, is beyond my physical endurance. I got up briskly. 'Don't you brood on these things too much,' I said. 'The thing you've got to do is to get out of this—get out of this sharp. You pull yourself together and *try.*'

"'I can't,' he said.

"'You try,' I said, and try he did."

"Try!" said Sanderson. "*How?*"

"Passes," said Clayton.

"Passes?"

"Complicated series of gestures and passes with the hands. That's how he had come in, and that's how he had to get out again. Lord! What a business I had!"

"But how could *any* series of passes—" I began.

"My dear man," said Clayton, turning on me and putting a great emphasis on certain words, "you want *everything* clear. I don't know *how.* All I know is that you *do*—that *he* did, anyhow, at least. After a fearful time, you know, he got his passes right and suddenly disappeared."

"Did you," said Sanderson slowly, "observe the passes?"

"Yes," said Clayton, and seemed to think. "It was tremendously queer," he said. "There we were, I and this thin, vague ghost, in that silent room, in this silent, empty inn, in this silent little Friday-night town. Not a sound except our voices and a faint panting he made when he swung. There was the bedroom candle, and one candle on the dressing table alight, that was all. Sometimes one or the other would flare up into a tall, lean, astonished flame for a space. And queer things happened. 'I can't,' he said. 'I shall never—' And suddenly he sat down on a little chair at the foot of the bed and began to sob and sob. Lord! What a harrowing, whimpering thing he seemed!

" 'You pull yourself together,' I said, and tried to pat him on the back, and . . . my confounded hand went through him! By that time, you know, I wasn't nearly so—massive as I had been on the landing. I got the queerness of it full. I remember snatching back my hand out of him, as it were, with a little thrill, and walking over to the dressing table. 'You pull yourself together,' I said to him, 'and try.' And in order to encourage and help him I began to try as well."

"What!" said Sanderson. "The passes?"

"Yes, the passes."

"But—" I said, moved by an idea that eluded me for a space.

"This is interesting," said Sanderson, with his finger in his pipe bowl. "You mean to say this ghost of yours gave way—"

"Did his level best to give away the whole confounded barrier? *Yes.*"

"He didn't," said Wish. "He couldn't. Or you'd have gone there, too."

"That's precisely it," I said, finding my elusive idea put into words for me.

"That *is* precisely it," said Clayton, with thoughtful eyes upon the fire.

For just a little while there was silence.

"And at last he did it?" said Sanderson.

"At last he did it. I had to keep him up to it hard, but he did it at last—rather suddenly. He despaired, we had a scene, and then he got up abruptly and asked me to go through the whole performance, slowly, so that he might see. 'I believe,' he said, 'if I could *see*, I should spot what was wrong at once.' And he did. '*I* know,' he said.

"'What do you know?' said I.

"'*I* know,' he repeated. Then he said, peevishly, 'I *can't* do it if you look at me—I really *can't;* it's been that, partly, all along. I'm such a nervous fellow that you put me out.'

"Well, we had a bit of an argument. Naturally I wanted to see; but he was as obstinate as a mule, and suddenly I had come over as tired as a dog—he tired me out. 'All right,' I said, '*I* won't look at you,' and turned toward the mirror on the wardrobe by the bed.

"He started off very fast. I tried to follow him by looking in the looking glass, to see just what it was had hung. Round went his arms and his hands, so, and so, and so, and then with a rush came to the last gesture of all—you stand erect and open out your arms—and so, don't you know, he stood. And then he didn't! He didn't! He wasn't! I wheeled round from the looking glass to him. There was nothing! I was alone, with the flaring candles and a staggering mind. What had happened? Had anything happened? Had I been dreaming? And then, with an absurd note of finality about it, the clock upon the landing discovered the moment was ripe for striking *one.* So! Ping! And I was as grave and sober as a judge, with all my champagne and whisky gone into the vast serene. Feeling queer, you know—confoundedly *queer!* Queer! Good Lord!"

He regarded his cigar ash thoughtfully for a moment. "That's all that happened," he said at last.

"And then you went to bed?" asked Evans.

"What else was there to do?"

I looked Wish in the eye. We wanted to scoff, and there was something, something perhaps in Clayton's voice and manner, that hampered our desire.

"And about these passes?" said Sanderson.

"I believe I could do them now."

"Oh!" said Sanderson, and produced a penknife and set himself to grub the dottel out of the bowl of his clay.

"Why don't you do them now?" said Sanderson, shutting his penknife with a click.

"That's what I'm going to do," said Clayton.

"They won't work," said Evans.

"If they do . . ." I suggested.

"You know, I'd rather you didn't," said Wish, stretching out his legs.

"Why?" asked Evans.

"I'd rather he didn't," said Wish.

"But he hasn't got 'em right," said Sanderson, plugging too much tobacco into his pipe.

"All the same, I'd rather he didn't," said Wish.

We argued with Wish. He said that for Clayton to go through those gestures was like mocking a serious matter. "But you don't believe—" I said.

Wish glanced at Clayton, who was staring into the fire, weighing something in his mind. "I do—more than half, anyhow, I do," said Wish.

"Clayton," said I, "you're too good a liar for us. Most of it was all right. But that disappearance . . . happened to be convincing. Tell us it's a tale of cock and bull."

He stood up without heeding me, took the middle of the hearthrug, and faced me. For a moment he regarded his feet thoughtfully, and then for all the rest of the time his eyes were on the opposite wall, with an intent expression.

He raised his two hands slowly to the level of his eyes and so began. . . .

Now, Sanderson is a Freemason, a member of the lodge of the Four Kings, which devotes itself so ably to the study and elucidation of all the mysteries of Masonry past and present, and among the students of this lodge Sanderson is by no means the least. He followed Clayton's motions with a singular interest in his reddish eye. "That's not bad," he said, when it was done. "You really do, you know, put things together, Clayton, in a most amazing fashion. But there's one little detail out."

"I know," said Clayton. "I believe I could tell you which."

"Well?"

"This," said Clayton, and did a queer little twist and writhing and thrust of the hands.

"Yes."

"That, you know, was what *he* couldn't get right," said Clayton. "But how do *you*—?"

"Most of this business, and particularly how you invented it, I don't understand at all," said Sanderson, "but just that phase—I do." He reflected. "These happen to be a series of gestures —connected with a certain branch of esoteric Masonry. Probably you know. Or else—*how?*" He reflected still further. "I do not see I can do any harm in telling you just the proper twist.

After all, if you know, you know; if you don't, you don't."

"I know nothing," said Clayton, "except what the poor devil let out last night."

"Well, anyhow," said Sanderson, and placed his churchwarden very carefully upon the shelf over the fireplace. Then very rapidly he gesticulated with his hands.

"So?" said Clayton, repeating.

"So," said Sanderson, and took his pipe in hand again.

"Ah, *now,*" said Clayton, "I can do the whole thing—right."

He stood up before the waning fire and smiled at us all. But I think there was just a little hesitation in his smile. "If I begin—" he said.

"I wouldn't begin," said Wish.

"It's all right!" said Evans. "Matter is indestructible. You don't think any jiggery-pokery of this sort is going to snatch Clayton into the world of shades. Not it! You may try, Clayton, so far as I'm concerned, until your arms drop off at the wrists."

"I don't believe that," said Wish, and stood up and put his arm on Clayton's shoulder. "You've made me half believe in that story somehow, and I don't want to see the thing done."

"Goodness!" said I. "Here's Wish frightened!"

"I am," said Wish, with real or admirably

feigned intensity. "I believe that if he goes through these motions right, he'll *go.* "

"He'll not do anything of the sort," I cried. "There's only one way out of this world for men, and Clayton is thirty years from that. Besides. . . . And such a ghost! Do you think—?"

Wish interrupted me by moving. He walked out from among the chairs and stopped beside the table and stood there. "Clayton," he said, "you're a fool."

Clayton, with a humorous light in his eyes, smiled back at him. "Wish," he said, "is right, and all you others are wrong. I shall go. I shall get to the end of these passes, and as the last swish whistles through the air, presto!—this hearthrug will be vacant, the room will be blank amazement, and a respectably dressed gentleman of fifteen stone will plump into the world of shades. I'm certain. So will you be. I decline to argue further. Let the thing be tried."

"*No,* " said Wish, and made a step and ceased, and Clayton raised his hands once more to repeat the spirit's passing.

By that time, you know, we were all in a state of tension—largely because of the behavior of Wish. We sat all of us with our eyes on Clayton —I, at least, with a sort of tight, stiff feeling about me as though from the back of my skull to the middle of my thighs my body had been changed to steel. And there, with a gravity that was imperturbably serene, Clayton bowed and swayed and waved his hands and arms before us. As he drew toward the end, one piled up, one tingled in one's teeth. The last gesture, I have said, was to swing the arms out wide open, with the face held up. And when at last he swung out to this closing gesture, I ceased even to breathe. It was ridiculous, of course, but you know that ghost-story feeling. It was after dinner, in a queer, old shadowy house. Would he, after all—?

There he stood for one stupendous moment, with his arms open and his upturned face, assured and bright, in the glare of the hanging lamp. We hung through that moment as if it were an age, and then came from all of us something that was half a sigh of infinite relief and half a reassuring *"No!"* For visibly—he wasn't going. It was all nonsense. He had told an idle story, and carried it almost to conviction, that was all! And then in that moment the face of Clayton changed.

It changed. It changed as a lit house changes when its lights are suddenly extinguished. His eyes were suddenly eyes that were fixed, his smile was frozen on his lips, and he stood there still. He stood there, very gently swaying.

That moment, too, was an age. And then, you

know, chairs were scraping, things were falling, and we were all moving. His knees seemed to give, and he fell forward, and Evans rose and caught him in his arms. . . .

It stunned us all. For a minute I suppose no one said a coherent thing. We believed it, yet could not believe it. . . . I came out of a muddled stupefaction to find myself kneeling beside him, and his vest and shirt were torn open, and Sanderson's hand lay on his heart. . . .

Well—the simple fact before us could very well wait our convenience; there was no hurry for us to comprehend. It lay there for an hour; it lies athwart my memory, black and amazing still, to this day. Clayton had, indeed, passed into the world that lies so near to and so far from our own, and he had gone thither by the only road that mortal man may take. But whether he did indeed pass there by that poor ghost's incantation, or whether he was stricken suddenly by apoplexy in the midst of an idle tale— as the coroner's jury would have us believe—is no matter for my judging; it is just one of those inexplicable riddles that must remain unsolved until the final solution of all things shall come. All I certainly know is that, in the very moment, in the very instant, of concluding those passes, he changed, and staggered, and fell down before us—dead!

WILLIAM HOPE HODGSON

The Whistling Room

Carnacki shook a friendly fist at me as I entered late. Then he opened the door into the dining room and ushered the four of us—Jessop, Arkright, Taylor, and me—in to dinner.

We dined well, as usual, and equally as usual Carnacki was pretty silent during the meal. At the end we took our wine and cigars to our accustomed positions, and Carnacki—having got himself comfortable in his big chair—began without any preliminary:

"I have just got back from Ireland again," he said. "And I thought you chaps would be interested to hear my news. Besides, I fancy I shall see the thing clearer after I have told it all out straight. I must tell you this, though, at the beginning: Up to the present moment I have been utterly and completely stumped. I have tumbled upon one of the most peculiar cases of haunting—or devilment of some sort—that I have come against. Now listen.

"I have been spending the last few weeks at

Iastrae Castle, about twenty miles northeast of Galway. I got a letter about a month ago from a Mr. Sid K. Tassoc, who it seemed had bought the place lately and moved in, only to find that he had got a very peculiar piece of property.

"When I reached there, he met me at the station and drove me up to the castle. I found that he was 'pigging it' there with his young brother and another American, who seemed to be half servant and half companion. It appears that all the servants had left the place, in a body as you might say, and now they were managing among themselves, assisted by some day help.

"The three of them got together a scratch feed, and Tassoc told me all about the trouble whilst we were at table. It is most extraordinary and different from anything that I have had to do with, though that Buzzing Case was very queer, too.

"Tassoc began right in the middle of his story. 'We've got a room in this shanty,' he said, 'which has got a most infernal whistling in it, sort of haunting it. The thing starts anytime, you never know when, and it goes on until it frightens you. It's not ordinary whistling, and it isn't the wind. Wait till you hear it.'

" 'We're all carrying guns,' said the boy, and slapped his coat pocket.

" 'As bad as that?' I said. The older brother

103

nodded. 'I may be soft,' he replied, 'but wait till you've heard it. Sometimes I think it's some infernal thing, and the next moment I'm just as sure that someone's playing a trick on us.'

"'Why?' I asked. 'What is to be gained?'

"'You mean,' he said, 'that people usually have some good reason for playing tricks as elaborate as this. Well, I'll tell you. There's a lady in this province, by the name of Miss Donnehue, who's going to be my wife, this day two months. She's more beautiful than they make them, and so far as I can see, I've just stuck my head into an Irish hornet's nest. There's about a score of hot young Irishmen been courting her these two years gone, and now that I've come along and cut them out, they feel raw against me. Do you begin to understand the possibilities?'

"'Yes,' I said. 'Perhaps I do in a vague sort of way, but I don't see how all this affects the room.'

"'Like this,' he said. 'When I'd fixed it up with Miss Donnehue, I looked out for a place and bought this one. Afterward I told her, one evening during dinner, that I'd decided to tie up here. And then she asked me whether I wasn't afraid of the whistling room. I told her it must have been thrown in gratis, as I'd heard nothing about it. There were some of her men friends present, and I saw a smile go round. I found out after a bit of questioning that several people have bought this place during the last twenty-odd years. And it was always on the market again, after a trial.

" 'Well, the chaps started to bait me a bit and offered to take bets after dinner that I'd not stay six months in this shanty. I looked once or twice at Miss Donnehue, but I could see that she didn't take it as a joke at all. Partly, I think, because there was a bit of a sneer in the way the men were tackling me, and partly because she really believed there was something in this yarn of the whistling room.

" 'However, after dinner I did what I could to even things up with the others. I nailed all their bets and screwed them down good and safe. I guess some of them are going to be hard hit, unless I lose, which I don't mean to. Well, there you have practically the whole yarn.'

" 'Not quite,' I told him. 'All I know is that you have bought a castle with a room in it that is in some way queer and that you've been doing some betting. Also, I know that your servants have got frightened and run away. Tell me something about the whistling.'

" 'Oh, that!' said Tassoc. 'That started the second night we were in. I'd had a good look round the room in the daytime, as you can understand, for the talk up at Arlestrae—Miss Donnehue's place—had me wonder a bit. But it seems just as usual as some of the other rooms in the old wing, only perhaps a bit more lonesome feeling. But that may be only because of the talk about it, you know.

" 'The whistling started about ten o'clock on the second night, as I said. Tom and I were in the library when we heard an awfully queer whistling coming along the east corridor—the room is in the east wing, you know.

" ' "That's that blessed ghost!" I said to Tom, and we collared the lamps off the table and went up to have a look. I tell you, even as we dug along the corridor, it took me a bit in the throat, it was so beastly queer. It was a sort of tune in a way, but more as if a devil or some rotten thing were laughing at you and going to get round at your back. That's how it makes you feel.

" 'When we got to the door, we didn't wait, but rushed it open, and then, I tell you, the sound of the thing fairly hit me in the face. Tom said he got it the same way—sort of felt stunned and bewildered. We looked all round and soon got so nervous we just cleared out, and I locked the door.

" 'We came down here and had a stiff drink each. Then we felt better and began to feel we'd

106

been nicely had. So we took sticks and went out into the grounds, thinking after all it must be some of these confounded Irishmen working the ghost trick on us. But there was nothing stirring.

"'We went back into the house and walked over it and then paid another visit to the room. But we simply couldn't stand it. We fairly ran out and locked the door again. I don't know how to put it into words, but I had a feeling of being up against something that was rottenly dangerous. You know! We've carried our guns ever since.

"'Of course, we had a real turnout of the room next day, and the whole house place, and we even hunted round the grounds, but there was nothing queer. And now I don't know what to think, except that the sensible part of me tells me that it's some plan of these wild Irishmen to try to take a rise out of me.'

"'Done anything since?' I asked him.

"'Yes,' he said. 'Watched outside the door of the room at night and chased round the grounds and sounded the walls and floor of the room. We've done everything we could think of, and it's beginning to get on our nerves, so we sent for you.'

"By this time we had finished eating. As we rose from the table, Tassoc suddenly called out, 'Ssh! Listen!'

"We were instantly silent, listening. Then I heard it, an extraordinary hooning whistle, monstrous and inhuman, coming from far away through corridors to my right.

"'By Heaven,' said Tassoc, 'and it's scarcely dark yet! Collar those candles, both of you, and come along.'

"In a few moments we were all out of the door and racing up the stairs. Tassoc turned into a long corridor, and we followed, shielding our candles as we ran. The sound seemed to fill all the passage as we drew near, until I had the feeling that the whole air throbbed under the power of some wanton, immense force—a sense of an actual taint, as you might say, of monstrosity all about us.

"Tassoc unlocked the door then, giving it a push with his foot, jumped back, and drew his revolver. As the door flew open the sound beat out at us with an effect impossible to explain to one who has not heard it—with a certain horrible personal note in it, as if in the darkness you could picture the room rocking and creaking in mad, vile glee to its own filthy piping and whistling and hooning, and yet all the time aware of you in particular. To stand there and listen was to be stunned by realization. It was as if someone showed you the mouth of a vast pit suddenly and said, 'That's Hell,' and you *knew* that they had spoken the truth. Do you get it, even a little bit?

"I stepped a pace into the room, held the candle over my head, and looked quickly round. Tassoc and his brother joined me, and the man came up at the back. We all held our candles high. I was deafened with the shrill, piping hoon of the whistling, and then, clear in my ear, something seemed to be saying to me: 'Get out of here—quick! Quick! Quick!'

"As you chaps know, I never neglect that sort of thing. Sometimes it may be nothing but nerves, but, as you will remember, it was just such a warning that saved me in the Grey Dog Case and in the Yellow Finger Experiments, as well as other times. Well, I turned sharp round to the others. 'Out!' I said. 'For the love of Heaven, *out, quick!*' And in an instant I had them into the passage.

"There came an extraordinary yelling scream into the hideous whistling and then, like a clap of thunder, an utter silence. I slammed the door and locked it. Then, taking the key, I looked round at the others. They were pretty white, and I imagine I must have looked that way, too. And there we stood a moment, silent.

" 'Come down out of this and have some whisky,' said Tassoc at last, in a voice he tried to make ordinary; and he led the way. I was the back man, and I knew we all kept looking over our shoulders. When we got downstairs, Tassoc passed the bottle round. He took a drink himself and slapped his glass onto the table, then sat down with a thud.

" 'That's a lovely thing to have in the house with you, isn't it!' he said. And directly afterward, 'What on earth made you hustle us all out like that, Carnacki?'

" 'Something seemed to be telling me to get out, *quick*,' I said. 'Sounds a bit silly—superstitious, I know—but when you are meddling with this sort of thing, you've got to take notice of queer fancies and risk being laughed at.'

"I told him about the Grey Dog business, and he nodded a lot to that. 'Of course,' I said, 'this may be nothing more than those would-be rivals of yours playing some funny game, but personally, though I'm going to keep an open mind, I feel that there is something beastly and dangerous about this thing.'

"We talked for a while longer, and then Tassoc suggested billiards, which we played in a pretty halfhearted fashion, all the time cocking an ear to the door for sounds. But none came, so later, after coffee, he suggested early bed and a thorough overhaul of the room in the morning.

"My bedroom was in the newer part of the

castle, and the door opened into the picture gallery. At the east end of the gallery was the entrance to the corridor of the east wing; this was shut off from the gallery by two old and heavy oak doors that looked rather odd and quaint beside the more modern doors of the various rooms.

"When I reached my room, I did not go to bed but began to unpack my instrument trunk. I intended to take one or two preliminary steps at once in my investigation of the extraordinary whistling.

"Presently, when the castle had settled into quietness, I slipped out of my room and across to the entrance of the great corridor. I opened one of the low, squat doors and threw the beam of my pocket searchlight down the passage. It was empty, and I went through the doorway and closed the oak behind me. Then along the great passageway, throwing my light before and behind and keeping my revolver handy.

"I had hung a 'protection belt' of garlic round my neck, and the smell of it seemed to fill the corridor and give me assurance; for, as you all know, it is a wonderful protection against the more usual Aeiirii forms of semimaterialization by which I supposed the whistling might be produced, though, at that period of my investigation, I was still quite prepared to find it due

111

to some perfectly natural cause. It is astonishing the enormous number of cases that prove to have nothing abnormal in them.

"In addition to wearing the necklet, I had plugged my ears loosely with garlic, and, as I did not intend to stay more than a few minutes in the room, I hoped to be safe.

"When I reached the door and put my hand into my pocket for the key, I had a sudden feeling of sickening funk. But I was not going to back out if I could help it. I unlocked the door and turned the handle. Then I gave the door a sharp push with my foot, as Tassoc had done, and drew my revolver, though I did not expect to have any use for it, really.

"I shone the searchlight all round the room and then stepped inside with a disgustingly horrible feeling of walking slap into a waiting danger. I stood a few seconds, expectant, and nothing happened, and the empty room showed bare from corner to corner. And then, you know, I realized that the room was full of purposeful silence, just as sickening as any of the filthy noises the things have power to make. Do you remember what I told you about the Silent Garden business? Well, this room had just that same *malevolent* silence—the beastly quietness of the thing that is looking at you and is not seeable itself and thinks that it has got you. Oh,

I recognized it instantly, and I slipped the top off my lantern so as to have light over the *whole* room.

"Then I set to working like fury and keeping my glance all about me. I sealed the two windows with lengths of human hair, right across, and sealed them at every frame. As I worked, a queer, scarcely perceptible tenseness stole into the air of the place, and the silence seemed, if you can understand me, to grow more solid. I knew then that I had no business there without full protection, for I was practically certain that this was no mere Aeiirii development, but one of the worse forms, such as the Saiitii—like that Grunting Man Case; you remember.

"I finished the windows and hurried over to the great fireplace. This is a huge affair and has a queer gallows-iron, I think they are called, projecting from the back of the arch. I sealed the opening with seven human hairs—the seventh crossing the six others.

"Then, just as I was making an end, a low, mocking whistle grew in the room. A cold, nervous prickling went up my spine and round my forehead from the back. The hideous sound filled the room with an extraordinary, grotesque parody of human whistling, too gigantic to be human—as if something gargantuan and monstrous made the sounds softly. As I stood

113

there a last moment, pressing down the final seal, I had little doubt but that I had come across one of those rare and horrible cases of the *inanimate* reproducing the functions of the *animate*. I made a grab for my lamp and went quickly to the door, looking over my shoulder and listening for the thing that I expected. It came just as I got my hand upon the handle— a squeal of incredible, malevolent anger, piercing through the low hooning of the whistling. I dashed out, slamming the door and locking it behind me.

"I leant a little against the opposite wall of the corridor, feeling rather funny, for it had been a hideously narrow squeak . . . 'thyr be noe sayfetie to be gained bye gayrds of holieness when the monyster hath pow'r to speak throe woode and stoene.' So runs the passage in the Sigsand manuscript, and I proved it in that Nodding Door business. There is no protection against this particular form of monster, except possibly for a fractional period of time, for it can reproduce itself in or take to its purposes the very protective material that you may use and has power to '*forme* wythine the pentycle,' though not immediately. There is, of course, the possibility of the Unknown Last Line of the Saaamaaa Ritual being uttered, but it is too uncertain to count upon, and the danger is too hideous, and even then it has no power to protect for more than 'maybe fyve beats of the harte' as the Sigsand has it.

"Inside of the room there was now a constant, meditative, hooning whistling, but presently this ceased, and the silence seemed worse, for there is such a sense of hidden mischief in a silence.

"After a little I sealed the door with crossed hairs and then cleared off down the great passage and so to bed.

"For a long time I lay awake but managed eventually to get some sleep. Yet about two o'clock I was waked by the hooning whistling of the room coming to me, even through the closed doors. The sound was tremendous and seemed to beat through the whole house with a presiding sense of terror. As if (I remember thinking) some monstrous giant had been holding mad carnival with itself at the end of that great passage.

"I got up and sat on the edge of the bed, wondering whether to go along and have a look at the seal, and suddenly there came a thump on my door, and Tassoc walked in, with his dressing gown over his pajamas.

"'I thought it would have waked you, so I came along to have a talk,' he said. 'I *can't* sleep. Beautiful! Isn't it?'

" 'Extraordinary!' I said, and tossed him my case.

"He lit a cigarette, and we sat and talked for about an hour, and all the time that noise went on down at the end of the big corridor.

"Suddenly Tassoc stood up.

" 'Let's take our guns and go and examine the brute,' he said, and turned toward the door.

" 'No!' I said. 'By Jove—NO! I can't say anything definite yet, but I believe that the room is about as dangerous as it well can be.'

" 'Haunted—*really* haunted?' he asked keenly and without any of his frequent banter.

"I told him, of course, that I could not say a definite yes or no to such a question, but that I hoped to be able to make a statement soon. Then I gave him a little lecture on the false rematerialization of the animate force through the inanimate-inert. He began then to understand the particular way in which the room might be dangerous, if it were really the subject of a manifestation.

"About an hour later the whistling ceased quite suddenly, and Tassoc went off again to bed. I went back to mine, also, and eventually got another spell of sleep.

"In the morning I walked along to the room. I found the seals on the door intact. Then I went in. The window seals and the hair were all right, but the seventh hair across the great fireplace was broken. This set me thinking. I knew that it might very possibly have snapped, through my having tensioned it too highly; but then, again, it might have been broken by something else. Yet it was scarcely possible that a man, for instance, could have passed between the six unbroken hairs, for no one would ever have noticed them, entering the room that way, you see—but would have just walked through them, ignorant of their very existence.

"I removed the other hairs and the seals. Then I looked up the chimney. It went up straight, and I could see blue sky at the top. It was a big, open flue and free from any suggestion of hiding places or corners. Yet, of course, I did not trust to any such casual examination, and after breakfast I put on my overalls and climbed to the very top, sounding all the way, but I found nothing.

"Then I came down and went over the whole of the room, floor, ceiling, and walls, mapping them out in six-inch squares and sounding with both hammer and probe. But there was nothing unusual.

"Afterward I made a three-week search of the whole castle in the same thorough way but found nothing. I went even further then, for at night, when the whistling commenced, I made a microphone test. You see, if the whistling were mechanically produced, this test would have made evident to me the working of the machinery, if there were any such concealed within the walls. It certainly was an up-to-date method of examination, as you must allow.

"Of course, I did not think that any of Tassoc's rivals had fixed up any mechanical contrivance, but I thought it just possible that there had been some such thing for producing the whistling, made away back in the years, perhaps with the intention of giving the room a reputation that would insure its being free of inquisitive folk. You see what I mean? Well, of course, it was just possible, if this were the case, that someone knew the secret of the machinery and was utilizing the knowledge to play this devil of a prank on Tassoc. The microphone test of the walls would certainly have made this known to me, as I have said, but there was nothing of the sort in the castle, so I had practically no doubt that it was a genuine case of what is popularly termed 'haunting.'

"All this time, every night and sometimes most of each night, the hooning whistling of the room was intolerable. It was as if an intelligence there knew that steps were being taken against it and piped and hooned in a sort of mad, mocking contempt. I tell you, it was as extraordinary as it was horrible. Time after time I went along—tiptoeing noiselessly on stockinged feet—to the sealed door (for I always kept the room sealed). I went at all hours of the night, and often the whistling inside would seem to change to a brutally jeering note, as though the half-animate monster saw me plainly through the shut door. And all the time, as I would stand watching, the hooning of the whistling would seem to fill the whole corridor, so that I used to feel a precious lonely chap messing about there with one of Hell's mysteries.

"And every morning I would enter the room and examine the different hairs and seals. You see, after the first week, I had stretched parallel hairs all along the walls of the room and along the ceiling, but over the floor, which was of polished stone, I had set out little colorless wafers, sticky side up. Each wafer was numbered and then arranged after a definite plan, so that I should be able to trace the exact movements of any living thing that went across.

"You will see that no material being or creature could possibly have entered that room without leaving many signs to tell me about it. But nothing was ever disturbed, and I began to think that I should have to risk an attempt to stay a night in the room in the Electric Pentacle.

Mind you, I *knew* that it would be a crazy thing to do, but I was getting stumped and ready to try anything.

"Once, about midnight, I did break the seal on the door and have a quick look in, but, I tell you, the whole room gave one mad yell and seemed to come toward me in a great billow of shadows, as if the walls had bellied in toward me. Of course, that must have been fancy. Anyway, the yell was sufficient, and I slammed the door and locked it behind me, feeling a bit weak down my spine. I wonder whether you know the feeling.

"And then, when I had got to that state of readiness for anything, I made what, at first, I thought was something of a discovery:

"'Twas about one in the morning, and I was walking slowly round the castle, keeping in the soft grass. I had come under the shadow of the east front, and far above me I heard the vile, hooning whistling of the room from up in the darkness of the unlit wing. Then suddenly, a little in front of me, I heard a man's voice speaking low, but evidently in glee.

"'By George, you chaps! I wouldn't care to bring a wife home to that!' it said, in the tone of the cultured Irish.

"Someone started to reply, but there came a sharp exclamation and then a rush, and I heard footsteps running in all directions. Evidently the men had spotted me.

"For a few seconds I stood there feeling an awful ass. After all, *they* were at the bottom of the haunting! Do you see what a big fool it made me seem? I had no doubt that they were some of Tassoc's rivals, and here I had been feeling in every bone that I had hit a genuine case! And then, you know, there came the memory of hundreds of details that made me just as much in doubt again. Anyway, whether it was natural or abnatural, there was a great deal yet to be cleared up.

"I told Tassoc next morning what I had discovered, and through the whole of every night for five nights we kept a close watch round the east wing, but there was never a sign of anyone prowling about; and all this time, almost endlessly from evening to dawn, that grotesque whistling would hoon incredibly, far above us in the darkness.

"On the morning after the fifth night, I received a wire from here that brought me home by the next boat. I explained to Tassoc that I was simply bound to go away for a few days but told him to keep up the watch round the castle. One thing I was very careful to do was to make him absolutely promise never to go into the room between sunset and sunrise. I made it

121

clear to him that we knew nothing definite yet, one way or the other, and if the room were what I had first thought it to be, it might be a lot better for him to die first rather than enter it after dark.

"When I got here and had finished my business, I thought you chaps would be interested, and also I wanted to get it all spread out clear in my mind, so I rang you up. I am going over again tomorrow, and when I get back, I ought to have something pretty extraordinary to tell you.

"By the way, there is a curious thing I forgot to tell you. I tried to get a phonographic record of the whistling, but it simply produced no impression on the wax at all. That is one of the things that has made me feel queer.

"Another extraordinary thing is that the microphone will not magnify the sound—will not even transmit it. Seems to take no account of it and acts as if it were nonexistent. I am absolutely and utterly stumped up to the present. I am a wee bit curious to see whether any of you dear clever heads can make daylight of it. *I* cannot—not yet."

He rose to his feet.

"Good night, all," he said, and began to usher us out abruptly, but without offense, into the night.

A fortnight later he dropped us each a card, and you can imagine that I was not late this time. When we arrived, Carnacki took us straight in to dinner, and when we had finished and all made ourselves comfortable, he began again, where he had left off:

"Now, just listen quietly, for I have got something very queer to tell you. I got back late at night, and I had to walk up to the castle, as I had not warned them that I was coming. It was bright moonlight, so that the walk was rather a pleasure than otherwise. When I got there, the whole place was in darkness, and I thought I would go round outside to see whether Tassoc or his brother was keeping watch. But I could not find them anywhere and concluded that they had got tired of it and gone off to bed.

"As I returned across the lawn that lies below the front of the east wing, I caught the hooning whistling of the room, coming down strangely clear through the stillness of the night. It had a peculiar note in it, I remember—low and constant, queerly meditative. I looked up at the window, bright in the moonlight, and got a sudden thought to bring a ladder from the stable yard and try to get a look into the room from the outside.

"With this notion I hunted round at the back of the castle among the straggle of the office and

presently found a long, fairly light ladder,
though it was heavy enough for one, goodness
knows! I thought at first that I should never get
it reared. I managed at last and let the ends rest
very quietly against the wall a little below the
sill of the larger window. Then, going silently,
I went up the ladder. Presently I had my face
above the sill and was looking in, alone with the
moonlight.

"Of course, the queer whistling sounded
louder up there, but it still conveyed that peculiar sense of something whistling quietly to itself
—can you understand? Though, for all the
meditative lowness of the note, the horrible,
gargantuan quality was distinct—a mighty
parody of the human, as if I stood there and
listened to the whistling from the lips of a
monster with a man's soul.

"And then, you know, I saw something. The
floor in the middle of the huge, empty room
was puckered upward in the center into a
strange, soft-looking mound, parted at the top
into an ever changing hole that pulsated to that
great, gentle hooning. At times, as I watched,
I saw the heaving of the indented mound gap
across with a queer, inward suction, as with
the drawing of an enormous breath, then the
thing would dilate and pout once more to the incredible melody. And suddenly as I stared,

dumb, it came to me that the thing was living. I was looking at two enormous, blackened lips, blistered and brutal, there in the pale moonlight.

"Abruptly they bulged out to a vast pouting mound of force and sound, stiffened and swollen and massive. And a great sweat lay heavy on the vast upper lip. In the same moment of time, the whistling had burst into a mad screaming note that seemed to stun me, even where I stood outside of the window. And then, the following moment, I was staring blankly at the solid, undisturbed floor of the room—smooth, polished stone flooring from wall to wall. And there was an absolute silence.

"You can picture me staring into the quiet room and knowing what I knew. I felt like a sick, frightened child, and I wanted to slide *quietly* down the ladder and run away. But in that very instant I heard Tassoc's voice calling to me from within the room for help! But I got such an awful dazed feeling, and I had a vague, bewildered notion that, after all, it was the Irishmen who had got him in there and were taking it out of him. And then the call came again, and I burst the window and jumped in to help him. I had a confused idea that the call had come from within the shadow of the great fireplace, but there was no one there.

"'Tassoc!' I shouted, and my voice went empty-sounding round the great apartment, and then in a flash *I knew that Tassoc had never called.* I whirled round, sick with fear, toward the window, and, as I did so, a frightful, exultant whistling scream burst through the room. On my left the end wall had bellied in toward me in a pair of gargantuan lips, black and utterly monstrous, to within a yard of my face. I fumbled for a mad instant at my revolver, not for *it,* but for myself, for the danger was a thousand times worse than death. And then, suddenly, the Unknown Last Line of the Saaamaaa Ritual was whispered quite audibly in the room. Instantly the thing happened that I have known once before. There came a sense as of dust falling continually and monotonously, and I knew that my life hung uncertain and suspended for a flash, in a brief, reeling vertigo of unseeable things. Then *that* ended, and I knew that I might live. My soul and body blended again, and life and power came to me. I dashed furiously at the window and hurled myself out headforemost, for I can tell you that I had stopped being afraid of death. I crashed down onto the ladder and slithered, grabbing and grabbing, and so came, someway or other, alive to the bottom. And there I sat in the soft, wet grass, with the moonlight all about me, and far above, through the broken window of the room, there was a low whistling.

"I was not hurt, and I went to the front and knocked. When they let me in, we had a long yarn over some good whisky—for I was shaken to pieces—and I explained things as much as I could. I told Tassoc that the room would have to come down and every fragment of it be burned in a blast furnace erected within a pentacle. He nodded. There was nothing to say. Then I went to bed.

"We turned a small army to the work, and within ten days that lovely thing had gone up in smoke, and what was left was calcined and clean.

"It was when the workmen were stripping the paneling that I got hold of a sound notion of the beginnings of that beastly development. Over the great fireplace, after the great oak panels had been torn down, I found that there was let into the masonry a scrollwork of stone with on it an old inscription in ancient Celtic: That here in this room was burned Dian Tiansay, Jester of King Alzof, who made the Song of Foolishness upon King Ernore of the Seventh Castle.

"When I got the translation clear, I gave it to Tassoc. He was tremendously excited, for he knew the old tale and took me down to the library to look at an old parchment that gave the story in detail. Afterward I found that the incident was well known about the countryside, but always regarded more as a legend than as history. And no one seemed ever to have dreamt that the old east wing of Iastrae Castle was the remains of the ancient Seventh Castle.

"From the old parchment I gathered that there had been a pretty dirty job done, away back in the years. It seems that King Alzof and King Ernore had been enemies by birthright, as you might say truly, but that nothing more than a little raiding had occurred on either side for years until Dian Tiansay made the Song of Foolishness upon King Ernore and sang it before King Alzof, and so greatly was it appreciated that King Alzof gave the jester one of his ladies to wife.

"Presently all the people of the land had come to know the song, and so it came at last to King Ernore, who was so angered that he made war upon his old enemy and took and burned him and his castle; but Dian Tiansay, the jester, he brought with him to his own place, and, having torn his tongue out because of the song that he had made and sung, he imprisoned him in the room in the east wing (which was evidently used for unpleasant purposes), and the jester's wife he kept for himself.

"But one night Dian Tiansay's wife was not to be found, and in the morning they discovered her lying dead in her husband's arms and him sitting whistling the Song of Foolishness, for he had no longer the power to sing it.

"Then they roasted Dian Tiansay in the great fireplace—probably from the selfsame gallows iron that I have already mentioned. And until he died, Dian Tiansay 'ceased not to whistle' the Song of Foolishness, which he could no longer sing. But afterward 'in that room' there was often heard at night the sound of something whistling, and there 'grew a power in that room,' so that none dared to sleep in it. And presently, it would seem, the King went to another castle, for the whistling troubled him.

"There you have it all. Of course, that is only a rough rendering of the translation from the parchment. It's a bit quaint! Don't you think so?"

"Yes," I said, answering for the lot. "But how did the thing grow to such a tremendous manifestation?"

"One of those cases of continuity of thought producing a positive action upon the immediate surrounding material," replied Carnacki. "The development must have been going forward through centuries, to have produced such a monstrosity. It was a true instance of the Saiitii

129

manifestation, best explained through likening it to a living spiritual fungus that involves the very structure of the ether fiber itself and, of course, in so doing, acquires an essential control over the material substance involved in it. It is impossible to make it plainer in a few words."

"Then you believe that the room itself had become the material expression of the ancient jester—that his soul, rotted with hatred, had bred into a monster—eh?" I asked.

"Yes," said Carnacki, nodding. "I think you've put my thought rather neatly. It is a queer coincidence that Miss Donnehue is supposed to be descended (so I heard since) from the same King Ernore. It makes one think some rather curious thoughts, doesn't it? The marriage coming on, and the room waking to fresh life. If she had gone into that room, ever . . . eh? IT had waited a long time. Sins of the fathers. Yes, I've thought of that. They're to be married next week, and I am to be best man, which is a thing I hate. And he won his bets, rather! Just think, *if* ever she had gone into that room—pretty horrible, eh?"

He nodded his head grimly, and we four nodded back. Then he rose and took us collectively to the door and presently thrust us forth in friendly fashion onto the Embankment and into the fresh night air.

"Good night," we called back and went to our various homes.

If she had, eh? If she had—that is what I kept thinking.

CARL JACOBI

The Last Drive

It was a cold wind that whipped across the hills that November evening. There was snow in the air, and Jeb Waters, in the cab of his jolting van, shivered and drew the collar of his sheep-skin higher about the throat. All day endless masses of white cumulus cloud had raced across a cheerless sky. They were gray now, those clouds, leaden gray, and so low-hanging that they seemed to lie like a pall on the crest of each distant hillock. Off to the right, stern and majestic, like a great parade of H. G. Wells's Martian creatures, marched the towers of the Eastern States Power lines, the only evidence here of present-day civilization. A low humming whine rose from the taut wires now, as the mounting wind twanged them in defiance.

Through the windshield Jeb Waters scanned the sky anxiously.

"It's going to be a cold trip back," he muttered to himself. "Looks mighty like a blizzard startin'."

He gave the engine a bit more gas and tightened his grasp on the wheel as a sharper curve loomed up suddenly before him. For a time he drove in silence, his mind fixed only on the barrenness of the hills on all sides. Marchester lay thirty miles ahead, thirty long, rolling miles. Littleton was just behind. If there were going to be a storm, perhaps it would be wise to return and wait until morning before making the trip. It would be bad to get stuck out here tonight, especially with the kind of load he was delivering. Enough to give one the creeps, even in the daytime.

Marchester, with its few hundred souls, hopelessly lost in the hills, too small or perhaps too lazy to incorporate itself, had been passed by without a glance when the railroad officials distributed spurs leading from the main line. As a result, all freight had to be trucked thirty miles across the country from Littleton, the nearest town on trackage. But there wasn't much freight, as the officials had suspected, and although Jeb Waters drove the distance only twice a week, he rarely returned with more than a single package.

Today, however, the load had stunned him with its importance. In the van, back of him, separated by only the wooden wall of the cab, lay a coffin, and in that coffin was the body of

Philip Carr, Marchester's most promising son. Philip Carr—Race Carr they had called him because he was such a driving fool—was the only man who could have brought the town to fame. With his queer-looking Speed Empress, the racing car that was a product of his own invention and three years' work, he had hoped to lower the automobile speed record on the sand track of Daytona Beach, Florida. He had clocked an unofficial 300 miles an hour in a practice attempt, and the world had sat up and taken notice.

On the fatal day, however, a tire had failed to stand the centrifugal force, and in a trice the car had twisted itself into a lump of steel. Philip Carr had been instantly killed. There was talk of burying him in Florida, but Marchester, his hometown, had absolutely refused. And so the body had been shipped back to Littleton, the nearest point on rails, and Jeb Waters had been sent to bring it from there to Marchester.

Jeb hadn't liked the idea. There was nothing to be afraid of, he knew, but somehow when he was alone in these Rentharpian Hills, even though he had known no other home since childhood, he always felt depressed and anxious for companionship. A coffin would hardly serve to ease his mind.

The wind was mounting steadily, and now

the first swirls of snow began to appear. The cab of the van was anything but warm. A corner of the windshield was broken out, and the rags Jeb had stuffed in the hole failed to keep out the cold.

Premature darkness had swooped down under the lowering clouds, and Jeb turned on the lights. The van was a very old one, and the lights worked on the magneto. As the snow became thicker and thicker, Jeb was forced to reduce his speed, and the lights, deprived of most of their current, dimmed to only a low, dismal glow, illuminating but little of the road that lay ahead.

Yet the miles rolled slowly by. The snow was piling in drifts now. It rolled across the hills, a great sweeping blanket of white, and swirled like powder through the crevices of the cab. And it was growing colder.

Frome's Hill, the steepest rise on the road, loomed up abruptly, and Jeb roared the rickety motor into a running start. The van lurched up the ascent, back wheels spinning in the soft snow, seeking traction. The engine hammered its protest. The transmission groaned as if in pain. Up, up climbed the truck, until at length it reached the very top.

"Now it's clear sailing," said Jeb aloud.

But he had spoken too soon. With a sigh, as if

the feat had been too great, the motor lapsed into sudden silence. The lights blinked out, and there was only the darkness of the hills and the swishing of the snow on the sides of the cab.

For a full moment Jeb sat there motionless as the horror of the situation fell upon him. Snowbound with a corpse! Twenty miles from the nearest habitation and alone with a coffin! A cold sweat burst out on his forehead at the realization of his predicament.

But he was acting like a child. It was ridiculous to let his nerves run away with him like that. If he could only keep from freezing, there would be no danger. In the morning, when it was found he hadn't reached Marchester, the people would send help.

Probably Ethan would come. Old Ethan. He would come in that funny sleigh of his, and he would say, "Well, Jeb, howdja like spending the night with a dead 'un?"

And then they would both laugh and drive back to town. . . . But that was tomorrow. Tonight there was the storm—and the corpse.

He set the spark, got out, and cranked the engine. But he did it halfheartedly. He knew by the tone of the engine when it had stopped that it would be a long time before it would resume revolutions.

At length he resigned himself to his plight,

returned to the cab, and tried to keep warm. But the cab was old and badly built. The wind blew through chinks and holes in great drafts, and snow sifted down his neck. It suddenly occurred to him that the back part of the van, which had been repaired recently, would give better protection against the blizzard than the cab. There were robes back there, too—robes used to keep packages from being broken. If only the coffin weren't there. One couldn't sleep next to it!

Another thought followed. Why not put the coffin in the cab? There was nothing else in the van, and he would then have the back of it to himself. He could lie down, too, and, with the robes, manage to keep warm somehow.

In a moment his mind was made up, and he set about to accomplish his task. It was hard, slow work. The coffin was heavy, the cab small, and the steering post in the way. Finally, by shoving it in end up, he managed it successfully, and then, going to the back of the van, he went in, closed the door, rolled up like a ball in the robes, and lay down to sleep.

Sleep proved elusive. He stirred restlessly, listening to the sounds of the storm. Occasionally the truck trembled as a stronger gust of wind struck it. Occasionally he could hear the mournful eolian whine of the power lines. Powdery snow rustled along the roof of the van. And the iron exhaust pipe cracked loudly as the heat left it. Minutes dragged by, slowly, interminably.

And then suddenly Jeb Waters sat bolt upright. Whether or not he had dozed off into a fitful sleep he did not know, but he was wide-awake now.

The van was moving! He could hear the tires crunching in the snow, could feel the slight swaying as the car gained momentum. He leaped to his feet and pressed his eyes against the little window that connected the back of the van with the cab.

For a moment he saw nothing. A strip of black velvet seemed pasted before the glass. Then the darkness softened. A soft glow seemed to form in the cab, and vaguely he seemed to see the figure of a man hunched over the wheel in the driver's position.

The van was going faster now. It creaked and swayed, and the wheels rumbled hollowly. Yet strangely enough there was no sound of the engine. Jeb hammered on the little pane of glass.

"Hey!" he cried. "Get away from that wheel! Stop!"

The figure seemed not to hear. With his hands grasping the wheel tightly, elbows far out, shoulders hunched low, he appeared aware of nothing but the dark road ahead of him.

Faster and faster sped the van.

Frantically Jeb rammed his clenched fist through the window. The glass broke into a thousand fragments.

"Do you hear?" he cried. "Stop, blast you! Stop!"

The man turned and leered at him. Even in the half glow Jeb recognized the features—that deathly white face, the black, glassy eyes.

"Oh, dear God," he screamed. *"It's Philip Carr!"* His voice rose to a hysterical, laughing sob. His hands trembled as he clutched the swaying walls, striving to keep his balance.

"Philip Carr," he shouted. "You're dead. You're dead, do you hear? You can't drive anymore."

A horrible, gurgling laugh came from the man at the wheel. The figure bent lower, as if to urge the van to a greater speed. And the van answered as if to a magic touch. On it raced into the storm, rocking and swaying like a thing accursed. Snow whirled past in great white clouds. The wind howled in maniacal accompaniment.

Suddenly, with a lurch, the van left the road and leaped toward the blacker shadows of a gully. A giant tree, its branches gesticulating wildly in the wind, reared up just ahead.

There came a crash!

"It's odd," said the coroner, and he frowned.

Old Ethan scratched his chin.

"It 'pears," he said, "as if that danged van engine went and stopped right on the top of that hill. Then Jeb, he musta gone into the back of the van to keep warm, and durin' the night the wind started the thing a-rollin'. It come tearin' down the hill, jumped into this here gully, and ran smash agin the tree. That's the way I figure it. Poor old Jeb!"

"Yes," replied the coroner, "but there doesn't seem to be the slightest injury on Jeb's body. Apparently he died of heart failure. And the corpse of Philip Carr! The crash might have ripped open the coffin, but that doesn't explain why the body, although set in rigor mortis, is in a sitting position. The way his arms are extended, it looks almost as though he were driving once more."

W. W. JACOBS

The Monkey's Paw

Without, the night was cold and wet, but in the small parlor of Lakesnam Villa, the blinds were drawn and the fire burned brightly. Father and son were at chess, the former, who possessed ideas about the game involving radical changes, putting his king into such sharp and unnecessary perils that it even provoked comment from the white-haired old lady knitting placidly by the fire.

"Hark at the wind," said Mr. White, who, having seen a fatal mistake after it was too late, was amiably desirous of preventing his son from seeing it.

"I'm listening," said the latter, grimly surveying the board as he stretched out his hand. "Check."

"I should hardly think that he'd come tonight," said his father, with his hand poised over the board.

"Mate," replied the son.

"That's the worst of living so far out," bawled

Mr. White, with sudden and unlooked-for violence. "Of all the beastly, slushy, out-of-the-way places to live in, this is the worst. Pathway's a bog, and the road's a torrent. I don't know what people are thinking about. I suppose, because only two houses on the road are let, they think the road doesn't matter."

"Never mind, dear," said his wife soothingly. "Perhaps you'll win the next one."

Mr. White looked up sharply, just in time to intercept a knowing glance between mother and son. The words died on his lips, and he hid a guilty grin in his thin gray beard.

"There he is," said Herbert White as the gate banged to loudly and heavy footsteps came toward the door.

The old man rose with hospitable haste and, opening the door, was heard condoling with the new arrival. The new arrival also condoled with himself, so that Mrs. White said, "Tut, tut!" and coughed gently as her husband entered the room, followed by a tall, burly man, beady of eye and rubicund of visage.

"Sergeant Major Morris," Mr. White announced.

The sergeant major shook hands and, taking the proffered seat by the fire, watched contentedly while his host got out whisky and tumblers and set a small copper kettle on the fire.

At the third glass, his eyes got brighter, and he began to talk, the little family circle regarding with eager interest this visitor from distant parts, as he squared his broad shoulders in the chair and spoke of strange scenes and doughty deeds, of wars and plagues and strange peoples.

"Twenty-one years of it," said Mr. White, nodding at his wife and son. "When he went away, he was a slip of a youth in the warehouse. Now look at him."

"He doesn't look to have taken much harm," said Mrs. White politely.

"I'd like to go to India myself," said the old man, "just to look around a bit, you know."

"Better where you are," said the sergeant major, shaking his head. He put down the empty glass and, sighing softly, shook his head again.

"I should like to see those old temples and fakirs and jugglers," said the old man. "What was that you started telling me the other day about a monkey's paw or something, Morris?"

"Nothing," said the soldier hastily. "Leastways, nothing worth hearing."

"Monkey's paw?" said Mrs. White curiously.

"Well, it's just a bit of what you might call magic, perhaps," said the sergeant major offhandedly.

His three listeners leaned forward eagerly. The visitor absentmindedly put his empty glass to his lips and then set it down again. His host filled it for him.

"To look at," said the sergeant major, fumbling in his pocket, "it's just an ordinary little paw, dried to a mummy."

He took something out of his pocket and proffered it. Mrs. White drew back with a grimace, but her son, taking it, examined it curiously.

"And what is there special about it?" inquired Mr. White as he took it from his son and, having examined it, placed it upon the table.

"It had a spell put on it by an old fakir," said the sergeant major, "a holy man. He wanted to show that fate ruled people's lives and that those who interfered with it did so to their sorrow. He put a spell on it so that three separate men could each have three wishes from it."

His manner was so impressive that his hearers were conscious that their light laughter jarred somewhat.

"Well, why don't you have three, sir?" said Herbert White cleverly.

The soldier regarded him in the way that middle age is wont to regard presumptuous youth. "I have," he said quietly, and his blotchy face whitened.

"And did you really have the three wishes granted?" asked Mrs. White.

"I did," said the sergeant major, and his glass

tapped against his strong teeth.

"And has anybody else wished?" inquired the old lady.

"The first man had his three wishes, yes," was the reply. "I don't know what the first two were, but the third was for death. That's how I got the paw."

His tones were so grave that a hush fell upon the group. "If you've had your three wishes, then it's not good to you now, Morris," said the old man at last. "What do you keep it for?"

The soldier shook his head. "Fancy, I suppose," he said slowly. "I did have some idea of selling it, but I don't think I will. It has caused enough mischief already. Besides, people won't buy. They think it's a fairy tale, some of them, and those who do think anything of it want to try it first and pay me afterward."

"If you could have another three wishes," said the old man, eyeing him keenly, "would you have them?"

"I don't know," said the other. "I don't know."

He took the paw and, dangling it between his front finger and thumb, suddenly threw it upon the fire. White, with a slight cry, stooped down and snatched it off.

"Better let it burn," said the soldier solemnly.

"If you don't want it, Morris," said the old man, "give it to me."

145

"I won't," said his friend doggedly. "I threw it on the fire. If you keep it, don't blame me for what happens. Pitch it on the fire again, like a sensible man."

The other shook his head and examined his new possession closely. "How do you do it?" he inquired.

"Hold it up in your right hand and wish aloud," said the sergeant major, "but I warn you of the consequences."

"Sounds like *The Arabian Nights,*" said Mrs. White as she rose and began to set the supper. "Don't you think you might wish for four pairs of hands for me?"

Her husband drew the talisman from his pocket, and then all three burst into laughter as the sergeant major, with a look of alarm on his face, caught him by the arm. "If you must wish," he said gruffly, "then wish for something sensible."

Mr. White dropped it back into his pocket and, placing chairs, motioned his friend to the table. In the business of supper the talisman was partly forgotten, and afterward the three Whites sat listening, enthralled, to a second installment of the soldier's adventures in India.

"If the tale about the monkey paw is not more truthful than those he has been telling us," said Herbert as the door closed behind their guest, just in time for him to catch the last train, "we shan't make much out of it."

"Did you give him anything for it, Father?" inquired Mrs. White, regarding her husband closely.

"A trifle," said he, coloring slightly. "He didn't want it, but I made him take it. And he pressed me again to throw it away."

"Likely!" said Herbert, with pretended horror. "Why, we're going to be rich and famous and happy. Wish to be an emperor, Father, to begin with; then you can't be henpecked."

He darted round the table, pursued by the maligned Mrs. White, who was armed with an antimacassar.

Mr. White took the paw from his pocket and eyed it dubiously. "I don't know what to wish for, and that's a fact," he said slowly. "It seems to me I've got all I want."

"If you only cleared the house, you'd be quite happy, wouldn't you?" said Herbert, putting his hand on his father's shoulder. "Well, wish for two hundred pounds, then; that will just do it, won't it?"

His father, smiling shamefacedly at his own credulity, held up the talisman as his son, with a solemn face somewhat marred by a wink at his mother, sat down at the piano and struck a few impressive chords.

"I wish for two hundred pounds," said the old man distinctly.

A fine crash from the piano greeted the words, interrupted by a shuddering cry from the old man. His wife and son ran toward him.

"It moved," he cried, with a glance of disgust at the object as it lay on the floor. "As I wished, it twisted in my hands like a snake."

"Well, I don't see the money," said his son as he picked the paw up and placed it on the table. "I bet I never shall."

"It must have been your fancy, Father," said his wife, regarding him anxiously.

He shook his head. "Never mind, though; there's no harm done, but it gave me a shock, all the same."

They sat down by the fire again, while the two men finished their pipes. Outside, the wind was higher than ever, and the old man started nervously at the sound of a door banging upstairs. A silence, unusual and depressing, settled upon all three, lasting until the old couple rose to retire for the night.

"I expect you'll find the cash tied up in a big bag in the middle of your bed," said Herbert as he bade them good night, "and something horrible squatting upon the top of the wardrobe, watching you as you pocket your ill-gotten gains."

Next morning, in the brightness of the wintry sun as it streamed over the breakfast table, Herbert laughed at his fears. There was an air of prosaic wholesomeness about the room, which it had lacked on the previous night, and the dirty, shriveled little paw was pitched on the sideboard with a carelessness that betokened no great belief in its virtues.

"I suppose all old soldiers are the same," said Mrs. White. "The idea of our listening to such nonsense! How could wishes be granted in these days? And if they could, how could two hundred pounds hurt you, Father?"

"Might drop on his head from the sky," said the frivolous Herbert.

"Morris said the things happened so naturally," said his father, "that you might, if you so wished, attribute them to coincidence."

"Well, don't break into the money before I come back," said Herbert as he rose from the table. "I'm afraid it'll turn you into a mean, avaricious man, and we shall have to disown you."

His mother laughed and followed him to the door. She watched him down the road and, returning to the breakfast table, was very happy at the expense of her husband's credulity. All of which did not prevent her from scurrying to the door at the postman's knock; nor did it

149

prevent her from referring rather shortly to
retired sergeant majors of bibulous habits whenever she found that the post had brought a
tailor's bill.

"Herbert will have some more of his funny
remarks, I expect, when he comes home," she
said as they sat at dinner.

"I daresay," said Mr. White, pouring himself
some beer, "but for all that, the thing moved in
my hand; that I'll swear to."

"You thought it did," said the old lady soothingly.

"I say it did," replied the other. "There was
no thought about it. I had just— What's the
matter?"

His wife made no reply. She was watching
the mysterious movements of a man outside,
who, peering in an undecided fashion at the
house, appeared to be trying to make up his
mind to enter.

Still mentally associated with the two hundred pounds, she noticed that the stranger was
well dressed, and that he wore a silk hat of
glossy newness.

Three times he paused at the gate and then
walked on again. The fourth time he stood with
his hand upon the gate and then, with sudden
resolution, flung it open and walked up the
path. Mrs. White placed her hands behind her,

and hurriedly unfastening the strings of her apron, put that useful article of apparel beneath the cushion of her chair.

She brought the stranger, who seemed ill at ease, into the room. He gazed furtively at Mrs. White and listened in a preoccupied fashion as the old lady apologized for the appearance of the room and her husband's coat, a garment that he usually reserved for the garden. She then waited, as patiently as her sex would permit, for him to broach his business, but he was at first strangely silent.

"I—was asked to call," he said at last, then stooped and picked a piece of cotton from his trousers. "I've come from Maw and Meggins."

The old lady started. "Is anything the matter?" she asked breathlessly. "Has anything happened to Herbert? What is it?"

Her husband interposed. "There, there, Mother," he said hastily. "Sit down, and don't jump to conclusions. You've not brought bad news, I'm sure, sir."

"I'm sorry—" began the visitor.

"Is he hurt?" demanded the mother.

The visitor bowed in assent. "Badly hurt," he said quietly, "but he is not in any pain."

"Oh, thank God!" said the old woman, clasping her hands tightly. "Thank God for that! Thank—"

She broke off suddenly as the sinister meaning of the assurance dawned upon her and she saw the awful confirmation of her fears in the other's averted face. She caught her breath, and turning to her slow-witted husband, laid her trembling old hand upon his. There was a long silence. Each was loath to pursue it further.

"He was caught in the machinery," said the visitor at length, in a low voice.

"Caught in the machinery," repeated Mr. White, in a dazed fashion, "yes."

He sat staring blackly out at the window, and taking his wife's hand between his own, pressed it as he had been wont to do in their old courting days nearly forty years before.

"He was the only one left to us," he said, turning gently to the visitor. "It is hard."

The other coughed and, rising, walked slowly to the window. "The firm wished me to convey their sincere sympathy in your great loss," he said, without looking around. "I beg that you will understand I am only their servant and merely obeying orders."

There was no reply. The old woman's face was white, her eyes staring and her breath inaudible; on the husband's face was a look such as his friend the sergeant might have carried into his first action.

"I was to say that Maw and Meggins disclaim

all responsibility," continued the other. "They admit no liability at all, but in consideration of your son's service, they wish to present you with a certain sum as compensation."

Mr. White dropped his wife's hand and, rising to his feet, gazed with a look of horror at his visitor. His dry lips shaped the words. "How much?"

"Two hundred pounds," was the answer.

Unconscious of his wife's shriek, the old man smiled faintly, put out his hand like a sightless man, and dropped, a senseless heap, to the floor.

In the huge new cemetery, some two miles distant, the old people buried their dead son and came back to a house steeped in shadow and silence.

It was all over so quickly that, at first, they could hardly realize it and remained in a state of expectation, as though of something else to happen—something else to happen—something else that was to lighten this load, too heavy for old hearts to bear.

But the days passed, and expectation gave place to resignation—the hopeless resignation of the old, sometimes miscalled apathy. Sometimes they hardly exchanged a word, for now they had nothing to talk about, and their days were long to weariness.

It was about a week after that that the old man, waking suddenly in the night, stretched out his hand and found himself alone. The room was in darkness, and the sound of subdued weeping came from the window. He raised himself in bed and listened.

"Come back," he said tenderly. "You will be cold."

"It is colder for my son," said the old woman, and she wept afresh.

The sound of her sobs died away on his ears. The bed was warm and his eyes heavy with sleep. He dozed fitfully and then slept, until a sudden wild cry from his wife awoke him with a start.

"The monkey's paw!" she cried wildly. "The monkey's paw!"

He started up in alarm. "Where? Where is it? What's the matter?"

She came stumbling across the room toward him. "I want it," she said quietly. "You've not destroyed it?"

"It's in the parlor, on the bracket," he replied, marveling. "Why?"

She cried and laughed together and, bending over, kissed his cheek.

"I only just thought of it," she said hysterically. "Why didn't I think of it before?"

"Think of what?" he questioned.

"The other two wishes," she replied rapidly. "We've only had one."

"Was not that enough?" he asked fiercely.

"No!" she cried triumphantly. "We'll have one more. Go down and get it quickly and wish our boy alive again!"

The man sat up in bed and flung the bed-clothes from his quaking limbs. "You are mad!" he cried, aghast.

"Get it," she panted, "get it quickly, and wish — Oh, my boy, my boy!"

Her husband struck a match and lit the candle. "Get back to bed," he said unsteadily. "You don't know what you are saying."

"We had the first wish granted," said the old woman feverishly. "Why not the second?"

"A coincidence," stammered the old man.

"Go and get it and wish," cried the old woman and dragged him toward the door.

He went down in the darkness and felt his way to the parlor and then to the mantelpiece. The talisman was in its place, and a horrible fear that the unspoken wish might bring his mutilated son before him ere he could escape from the room seized upon him, and he caught his breath as he found that he had lost the direction of the door. His brow cold with sweat, he felt his way round the table and groped along the wall until he found himself in the small

155

passage, with the unwholesome thing in his hand.

Even his wife's face seemed changed as he entered the room. It was white and expectant and, to his fears, seemed to have an unnatural look upon it. He was afraid of her.

"Wish!" she cried, in a strong voice.

"It is foolish and wicked," he faltered.

"Wish!" repeated his wife.

He raised his hand. "I wish my son alive again."

The talisman fell to the floor, and he regarded it shudderingly. Then he sank, trembling, into a chair as the old woman, with burning eyes, walked to the window and raised the blind.

He sat until he was chilled with the cold, glancing occasionally at the figure of the old woman peering through the window. The candle end, which had burnt below the rim of the china candlestick, was throwing pulsating shadows on the ceiling and walls, until, with a flicker larger than the rest, it expired.

The old man, with an indescribable sense of relief at the failure of the talisman, crept back to his bed, and a minute or two afterward the old woman came silently and apathetically beside him.

Neither spoke, but both lay silent, listening to the ticking of the clock. A stair creaked, and a squeaky mouse scurried noisily through the wall. The darkness was oppressive, and, after lying for some time screwing up his courage, the husband took the box of matches and, striking one, went downstairs for a candle.

At the foot of the stairs the match went out, and he paused to strike another, and at the same moment a knock, so quiet and stealthy as to be scarcely audible, sounded on the front door.

The matches fell from his hand. He stood motionless, his breath suspended, until the knock was repeated. Then he turned and fled swiftly back to his room and closed the door behind him. A third knock sounded through the house.

"What's that?" cried the woman, starting up.

"A rat," said the old man, in shaking tones, "a rat. It passed me on the stairs."

His wife sat up in bed listening. A loud knock resounded through the house.

"It's Herbert! It's Herbert!"

She ran to the door, but her husband was before her, and, catching her by the arm, he held her tightly.

"What are you going to do?" he whispered hoarsely.

"It's my boy; it's Herbert!" she cried, struggling mechanically. "I forgot it was miles away.

What are you holding me for? Let go. I must open the door."

"Please God, don't let it in," cried the old man, trembling.

"You're afraid of your own son," she cried, struggling. "Let me go. I'm coming, Herbert; I'm coming!"

There was another knock, and another. The old woman, with a sudden wrench, broke free and ran from the room. Her husband followed to the landing and called after her appealingly as she hurried downstairs. He heard the chain rattle back and the bottom bolt drawn slowly and stiffly from the socket. Then the old woman's voice was heard, strained and panting.

"The bolt," she cried loudly. "Come down. I can't reach it."

But her husband was on his hands and knees, groping wildly on the floor in search of the paw. If he could only find it before the thing outside got in! A perfect fusillade of knocks reverberated through the house, and he heard the scraping of a chair as his wife put it down in the passage against the door. He heard the creaking of the bolt as it came slowly back, and at the same moment he found the monkey's paw and frantically breathed his third and last wish.

The knocking ceased suddenly, although the echoes of it were still in the house. He heard the chair being drawn back and the door being opened. A cold wind rushed up the staircase, and a long, loud wail of disappointment and misery from his wife gave him courage to run down to her side and then to the gate beyond. The street lamp flickering opposite shone on a quiet and deserted road.

FRANK BELKNAP LONG

Second Night Out

It was past midnight when I left my stateroom. The upper promenade deck was entirely deserted, and thin wisps of fog hovered about the deck chairs and curled and uncurled about the gleaming rails. No air was stirring. The ship moved forward sluggishly through a quiet, fog enshrouded sea.

But I did not object to the fog. I leaned against the rail and inhaled the damp, murky air with a positive greediness. The almost unendurable nausea, the pervasive physical and mental misery had departed, leaving me serene and at peace. I was again capable of experiencing sensuous delight, and the aroma of the brine was not to be exchanged for pearls and rubies. I had paid in exorbitant coinage for what I was about to enjoy—for the five brief days of freedom and exploration in glamorous, sea-splendid Havana, which I had been promised by an enterprising and, I hoped, reasonably honest tourist agent. I am in all respects the antithesis of a wealthy man, and I had drawn so heavily upon my bank balance to satisfy the greedy demands of The Loriland Tours, Inc., that I had been compelled to renounce such really indispensable amenities as after-dinner cigars and ocean-privileged sherry and chartreuse.

But I was enormously content. I paced the deck and inhaled the moist, pungent air. For thirty hours I had been confined to my cabin with a sea illness more debilitating than bubonic plague or malignant sepsis, but having at length managed to squirm from beneath its iron heel, I was free to enjoy my prospects. They were enviable and glorious. Five days in Cuba, with the privilege of driving up and down the sun-drenched Malecon in a flamboyantly upholstered limousine, and an opportunity to feast my discerning gaze on the pink walls of the cabanas and the Columbus Cathedral and La Fuerza, the great storehouse of the Indies. Opportunity, also, to visit sunlit patios, saunter by iron-barred *rejas,* sip *refrescos* by moonlight in open-air cafés, and acquire, incidentally, a Spanish contempt for Big Business and the Strenuous Life. Then to Haiti, dark and magical; the Virgin Islands and the quaint, incredible Old World harbor of Charlotte Amalie, with its chimneyless, red-roofed houses rising in tiers to the quiet stars; the natural Sargasso, the inevitable last port of call for rainbow fishes, diving boys, old ships with sun bleached funnels, and incurably drunken skippers. A flaming opal set in an amphitheater of malachite—its allure blazed forth through the gray fog and dispelled my northern spleen. I leaned against the rail and dreamed also of Martinique, which I would see in a few days, and of the Indian and Chinese wenches of Trinidad. And then, suddenly, a dizziness came upon me. The ancient and terrible malady had returned to plague me.

Seasickness, unlike all other major afflictions, is a disease of the individual. No two people are ever afflicted with precisely the same symptoms. The manifestations range from a slight malaise to a devastating impairment of all one's faculties. I was afflicted with the gravest symptoms imaginable. Choking and gasping, I left the rail and sank helplessly down into one of the three remaining deck chairs.

Why the steward had permitted the chairs to remain on deck was a mystery I couldn't fathom. He had obviously shirked a duty, for passengers did not habitually visit the promenade deck in the small hours, and foggy weather plays havoc with the wickerwork of steamer chairs. But I was too grateful for the benefits that his negligence had conferred upon me to be excessively critical. I lay sprawled at full length, grimacing and gasping and trying fervently to assure myself that I wasn't nearly as sick as I felt. And then, all at once, I became aware of an additional source of discomfiture.

The chair exuded an unwholesome odor. It was unmistakable. As I turned about, and as my cheek came to rest against the damp, varnished wood, my nostrils were assailed by an acrid and alien odor of a vehement, cloying potency. It was at once stimulating and indescribably repellent. In a measure, it assuaged my physical unease, but it also filled me with the most overpowering revulsion—with a sudden, hysterical, and almost frenzied distaste.

I tried to rise from the chair, but the strength was gone from my limbs. An intangible presence seemed to rest upon me and weigh me down. And then the bottom seemed to drop out of everything. I am not being facetious. Something of the sort actually occurred. The *base* of the sane, familiar world vanished, was swallowed up. I sank down. Limitless gulfs seemed open beneath me, and I was immersed, lost in a gray void. The ship, however, did not vanish. The ship, the deck, the chair continued to support me, and yet, despite the retention of these outward symbols of reality, I was afloat in an unfathomable void. I had the illusion of falling, of sinking helplessly through an eternity of space. It was as though the deck chair that supported me had passed into another dimension without ceasing to leave the familiar world —as though it floated simultaneously both in our three-dimensional world and in another world of alien, unknown dimensions. I became aware of strange shapes and shadows all about me. I gazed through illimitable dark gulfs at continents and islands, lagoons, atolls, vast gray waterspouts. I sank down into the great deep. I was immersed in dark slime. The boundaries of sense were dissolved away, and the breath of an active corruption blew through me, gnawing at my vitals and filling me with extravagant torment. I was alone in the great deep. And the shapes that accompanied me in my utter abysmal isolation were shriveled and black and dead, and they cavorted deliriously with little monkey heads with streaming, sea-drenched viscera and putrid, pupilless eyes.

And then, slowly, the unclean vision dissolved. I was back again in my chair, and the fog was as dense as ever, and the ship moved forward steadily through the quiet sea. But the odor was still present—acrid, overpowering, revolting. I leapt from the chair in profound alarm. I experienced a sense of having emerged from the bowels of some stupendous and unearthly *encroachment*—of having, in a single instant, exhausted the resources of earth's malignity and drawn upon untapped and intolerable reserves.

I have gazed without flinching at the turbulent, demon-seething, utterly benighted infernos of the Italian and Flemish primitives. I have endured with calm vision the major inflictions of Hieronymus Bosch and Lucas Cranach, and I have not quailed even before the worst perversities of the elder Breughel, whose outrageous gargoyles and ghouls and cacodemons are so self-contained that they fester with an overbrimming malignancy and seem about to burst asunder and dissolve hideously in a black and intolerable froth. But not even Signorelli's *Soul of the Damned,* or *Goya's Los Caprichos,* or the hideous, ooze-encrusted sea-shapes with half-assembled bodies and dead, pupilless eyes, which drag themselves sightlessly through Segrelles' blue worlds of fetor and decay were as unnerving and ghastly as the flickering visual sequence that had accompanied my perception of the odor. I was vastly and terribly shaken.

I got indoors somehow, into the warm and steamy interior of the upper saloon, and waited, gasping, for the deck steward to come to me. I had pressed a small button labeled DECK STEWARD in the wainscoting adjoining the central stairway, and I frantically hoped that he would arrive before it was too late, before the odor outside percolated into the vast, deserted saloon.

The steward was a daytime official, and it was a cardinal crime to fetch him from his berth at one in the morning, but I had to have someone to talk to, and as the steward was responsible for the chairs, I naturally thought of him as the logical target for my interrogations. He would *know.* He would be able to explain. The odor would not be unfamiliar to him. He would be able to explain about the chairs . . . about the chairs . . . about the chairs. . . . I was growing hysterical and confused.

I wiped the perspiration from my forehead with the back of my hand and waited with relief for the steward to approach. He had come suddenly into view above the top of the central stairway, and he seemed to advance toward me through a blue mist.

He was extremely solicitous, extremely courteous. He bent above me and laid his hand concernedly upon my arm. "Yes, sir. What can I do for you, sir? A bit under the weather, perhaps? What can I do?"

Do? Do? It was horribly confusing. I could only stammer, "The chairs, steward. On the deck. Three chairs. Why did you leave them there? Why didn't you take them inside?"

It wasn't what I had intended asking him. I had intended questioning him about the odor. But the strain, the shock had confused me. The first thought that came into my mind on seeing the steward standing above me, so solicitous and concerned, was that he was a hypocrite and a scoundrel. He pretended to be concerned about me, and yet, out of sheer perversity, he had prepared the snare that had reduced me to a pitiful and helpless wreck. He had left the chairs on deck deliberately, with a cruel and crafty malice, knowing all the time, no doubt, that *something* would occupy them.

But I wasn't prepared for the almost instant change in the man's demeanor. It was ghastly. Befuddled as I had become, I could perceive at once that I had done him a grave, terrible injustice. *He hadn't known.* All the blood drained out of his cheeks, and his mouth fell open. He stood immobile before me, completely inarticulate, and, for an instant, I thought he was about to collapse helplessly down upon the floor.

"You saw—chairs?" he gasped at last.

I nodded.

The steward leaned toward me and gripped my arm. The flesh of his face was completely destitute of luster. From the parchment-white oval his two eyes, tumescent with fright, stared wildly down at me.

167

"It's the black, dead thing," he muttered. "The monkey face. I *knew* it would come back. It always comes aboard at midnight on the second night out."

He gulped and his hand tightened on my arm.

"It's always on the second night out. It knows where I keep the chairs, and it takes them on deck and sits in them. I *saw* it last time. It was squirming about in the chair—lying stretched out and squirming horribly. Like an eel. It sits in all three of the chairs. When it saw me, it got up and started toward me. But I got away. I came in here and shut the door. But I saw it through the window."

The steward raised his arm and pointed.

"There. Through that window there. Its face was pressed against the glass. It was all black and shriveled and eaten away. A monkey face, sir. So help me, the face of a dead, shriveled monkey. And wet—dripping. I was so frightened I couldn't breathe. I just stood and groaned, and then it went away."

He gulped.

"Dr. Blodgett was mangled, clawed to death, at ten minutes to one. We heard his shrieks. The thing went back, I guess, and sat in the chairs for thirty or forty minutes after it left the window. Then it went down to Dr. Blodgett's stateroom and took his clothes. It was horrible.

Dr. Blodgett's legs were missing, and his face was crushed to a pulp. There were claw marks all over him. And the curtains of his berth were drenched with blood.

"The captain told me not to talk. But I've got to tell someone. I can't help myself, sir. I'm afraid—I've got to talk. This is the third time it's come aboard. It didn't take anybody the first time, but it sat in the chairs. It left them all wet and slimy, sir—all covered with black, stinking slime."

I stared in bewilderment. What was the man trying to tell me? Was he completely unhinged? Or was I too confused, too ill myself to catch all that he was saying?

He went on wildly. "It's hard to explain, sir, but this boat is *visited*. Every voyage, sir—on the second night out. And each time it sits in the chairs. Do you understand?"

I didn't understand clearly, but I murmured a feeble assent. My voice was appallingly tremulous, and it seemed to come from the opposite side of the saloon.

"Something out there," I gasped. "It was awful. Out there, you hear? An awful odor. My brain. I can't imagine what's come over me, but I feel as though something were pressing on my brain. Here."

I passed my fingers across my forehead.

169

"Something here—something—"

The steward appeared to understand perfectly. He nodded and helped me to my feet. He was still self-engrossed, still horribly wrought up, but I could sense that he was also anxious to reassure and assist me.

"Stateroom Sixteen D? Yes, of course. Steady, sir."

The steward had taken my arm and was guiding me toward the central stairway. I could scarcely stand erect. My decrepitude was so apparent, in fact, that the steward was moved by compassion to the display of an almost heroic attentiveness. Twice I stumbled and would have fallen had not the guiding arm of my companion encircled my shoulders and levitated my sagging bulk.

"Just a few more steps, sir. That's it. Just take your time. There isn't anything will come of it, sir. You'll feel better when you're inside, with the fan going. Just take your time, sir."

At the door of my stateroom, I spoke in a hoarse whisper to the man at my side. "I'm all right now. I'll ring if I need you. Just—let me—get inside. I want to lie down. Does this door lock from the inside?"

"Why, yes. Yes, of course. But maybe I'd better get you some water."

"No, don't bother. Just leave me—please."

"Well—all right, sir." Reluctantly the steward departed.

The stateroom was extremely dark. I was so weak that I was compelled to lean with all my weight against the door to close it. It shut with a slight click, and the key fell out upon the floor. With a groan I went down on my knees and groveled apprehensively on the soft carpet. But the key eluded me.

I cursed and was about to rise, when my hand encountered something fibrous and hard. I started back, gasping. Then, frantically, my fingers slid over it, in a hectic effort at appraisal. It was—yes, undoubtedly, a shoe. And sprouting from it, an ankle. The shoe stood firmly on the floor of the stateroom. The flesh of the ankle, beneath the sock that covered it, was very cold.

In an instant I was on my feet, circling like a caged animal about the narrow dimensions of the stateroom. My hands slid over the walls, the ceiling. If only, dear God, the electric light button would not continue to elude me!

Eventually my hands encountered a rubbery excrescence on the smooth panel. I pressed resolutely, and the darkness vanished to reveal a man sitting upright on a couch in the corner— a stout, well-dressed man, holding a grip and looking perfectly composed. Only his face was

171

invisible. His face was concealed by a handkerchief—a large handkerchief that had obviously been placed there intentionally, perhaps as a protection against the rather chilly air currents from the unshuttered port. The man was obviously asleep. He had not responded to the tugging of my hands on his ankles in the darkness, and even now he did not stir. The glare of the electric light bulbs above his head did not appear to annoy him in the least.

I experienced a sudden and overwhelming relief. I sat down beside the intruder and wiped the sweat from my forehead. I was still trembling in every limb, but the calm appearance of the man beside me was tremendously reassuring. A fellow passenger, no doubt, who had entered the wrong compartment. It should not be difficult to get rid of him. A mere tap on the shoulder, followed by a courteous explanation, and the intruder would vanish. A simple procedure, if only I could summon the strength to act with decision. I was so horribly enfeebled, so incredibly weak and ill. But at last I mustered sufficient energy to reach out my hand and tap the intruder on the shoulder.

"I'm sorry, sir," I murmured, "but you've got into the wrong stateroom. If I weren't a bit under the weather, I'd ask you to stay and smoke a cigar with me, but, you see, I—" with a distorted effort at a smile I tapped the stranger again nervously—"I'd rather be alone, so if you don't mind—sorry I had to wake you."

Immediately I perceived that I was being premature. I had not waked the stranger. The stranger did not budge, did not so much as agitate by his breathing the handkerchief that concealed his features.

I experienced a resurgence of my alarm. Tremulously I stretched forth my hand and seized a corner of the handkerchief. It was an outrageous thing to do, but I had to know. If the intruder's face matched his body, if it was composed and familiar, all would be well, but if for any reason—

The fragment of physiognomy revealed by the uplifted corner was not reassuring. With a gasp of fright I tore the handkerchief completely away. For a moment, a moment only, I stared at the dark and repulsive visage, with its stary, corpse-white eyes, viscid and malignant, its flat simian nose, hairy ears, and thick black tongue that seemed to leap up at me from out of the mouth. The face *moved* as I watched it, wriggled and squirmed revoltingly, while the head itself shifted its position, turning slightly to one side and revealing a profile even more bestial and gangrenous and unclean than the brunt of its countenance.

I shrank back against the door in frenzied dismay. I suffered as an animal suffers. My mind, deprived by shock of all capacity to form concepts, agonized instinctively, at a brutish level of consciousness. Yet, through it all, one mysterious part of myself remained horribly observant. I saw the tongue snap back into the mouth; saw the lines of the features shrivel and soften, until presently, from the slavering mouth and white, sightless eyes, there began to trickle thin streams of blood. In another moment the mouth was a red slit in a splotched horror of countenance—a red slit rapidly widening and dissolving in an amorphous crimson flood. The horror was hideously and repellently dissolving into the basal sustainer of all life.

It took the steward nearly ten minutes to restore me. He was compelled to force spoonfuls of brandy between my tightly locked teeth, to bathe my forehead with ice water, and to massage, almost savagely, my wrists and ankles. And when finally I opened my eyes, he refused to meet them. He quite obviously wanted me to rest, to remain quiet, and he appeared to distrust his own emotional equipment. He was good enough, however, to enumerate the measures that had contributed to my restoration and to enlighten me in respect to the *remnants*.

"The clothes were all covered with blood—*drenched*, sir. I burned them."

On the following day he became more loquacious. "It was wearing the clothes of the gentleman who was killed last voyage, sir—it was wearing Dr. Blodgett's things. I recognized them instantly."

"But, why—"

The steward shook his head. "I don't know, sir. Maybe your going up on deck saved you. Maybe it couldn't wait. It left a little after the last time, sir, and it was later than that when I saw you to your stateroom. The ship may have passed out of its zone, sir. Or maybe it fell asleep and couldn't get back in time, and that's why it—dissolved. I don't think it's gone for good. There was blood on the curtains in Dr. Blodgett's cabin, and I'm afraid it always goes that way. It will come back next voyage, sir. I'm sure of it."

He cleared his throat.

"I'm glad you rang for me. If you'd gone right down to your stateroom, it might be wearing your clothes next voyage."

Havana failed to restore me. Haiti was a black horror, a repellent quagmire of menacing shadows and alien desolation, and in Martinique I did not get a single hour of undisturbed sleep in my room at the hotel.

175

ROBERT G. ANDERSON

The Hills Beyond Furcy

The party had passed its peak. Tienne, the tall, enigmatic exchange student from Haiti, surveyed the half dozen couples, college classmates all, who were gyrating tiredly in various versions of the Swim, the Jerk, or the Gorilla.

Dave Grayden's apartment was crowded, filled with body heat, and hazy with smoke, a contrast to the February wind that lashed at the windows. Tienne stood in a darkened alcove, aloof, remote; his intense gaze riveted on Carol Braun—no—Carol Mason, now that she and Roger were married.

The Roger Masons, guests at this informal discotheque, were to leave in two days on a delayed honeymoon to the Caribbean—delayed because of Roger's graduation. But it had been worth waiting for, because even before his graduation in the top ten of his class in chemical engineering, job offers had poured in on him. He finally chose Fraser Oil, which offered an excellent starting salary and the chance for rapid advancement. They also had given him a generous bonus for signing, plus a month's grace before reporting for work.

Someone turned the record player down and called out in a thick voice, "Tienne, how about some of your voodoo? You know, that ol' black magic."

A flicker of annoyance darted across the dark, handsome features of the Haitian. He tried to ignore the request, but others took it up; they were tired of dancing.

"Show us some magic. Show us some voodoo from Haiti."

The dancing stopped altogether, and the record player turned itself off. The group eyed Tienne expectantly, hoping he'd respond.

Chick Melardi, bold and brash as always, scoffed, "Voodoo! That mumbo-jumbo! Jumping around the place and killing chickens. Oh, brother!"

But he was the lone dissenter; the others hooted him down. Chick's words stung Tienne, and his lips tightened. The fact that he had one too many of Dave's Specials also made him a little reckless. A wry smile played about his lips. He shrugged and held up a hand.

"All right, what do you want?"

He stepped to the middle of the room, and the couples fell back into a ragged circle. Tienne stood alone, a bold, striking figure in a dark business suit. His eyes held darting yellow lights in their depths, lights that lashed like the tail of a wild thing.

Carol and Roger pressed forward with the rest, and Roger's thoughts went back two years, to when Tienne had first arrived at the university. From the day when he had accidentally dumped a bowl of bean soup into Carol's lap in the crush of a busy cafeteria, they had formed an unusual triumvirate on campus. It was Carol who had taught the Haitian student the intricacies of American slang, and how much catsup and/or mustard was proper on a Campus-Union hamburger.

Carol's courses were in the humanities, far removed from the scientific chemical engineering of Roger and Tienne. She told Roger that, surprisingly, Tienne had a remarkable insight into poetry and philosophy. If Roger felt a twinge of jealousy at this, he was comforted by the knowledge that he and Carol would be married just as soon as he graduated. They did get married, and although Tienne knew how it was with them, he continued to gaze at her with his wise, old-young, sad, adoring eyes.

Carol was the target of Tienne's eyes now, as he stood alone, the air charged and electric about him. Carol turned her eyes away.

Impish little Donna Lennart, giggling, suggested, "I'll tell you what, Tienne. Get Dave, here, to shut up, for a starter. He's been bending my ear all evening about his canoe trip in British Columbia last summer; what a bore!"

"Hey, you can't say things like that about your boyfriend. Besides, I've got so much money that everything I say should be fascinating."

There was laughter at this, but Tienne held up a hand again, and the room quieted by stages. His voice was commanding.

"You!" He indicated Morrie Day, a devotee of the bongos. "Take this beat!" He rapped a staccato series on the edge of the side table. To the others, "Be quiet, and observe."

Morrie carried the pair of bongos from a corner, sat down, and clasped them between his knees. Soon the room was pervaded with a sound like the thumping of a wild heart.

From an inside pocket, Tienne took a small package wrapped in what looked like a dirty rag. Carefully he unrolled it and revealed three dried chicken bones, several short, hollow sticks, and a few white feathers. The feathers were dotted with dark blots. Dried blood? The wild drumming subsided to a hum, and Tienne placed the bundle on the floor and began a slow shuffle around it. There was an intense look on his face as he began an unintelligible chant, a curious mixture of French patois and African. Roger caught the word "Malele" recurring time and again.

Once, Tienne stopped his shuffling dance and, squatting, quickly and accurately drew a portrait of a man on the rug by dribbling sand from his fingers. It was a likeness of Dave. As he finished, Tienne drew a final line across the throat of the picture. Then he straightened, resuming his shuffling dance and chant. The spectators were engulfed in rhythm as his voice rose and fell, the words weaving around the drumbeats. The throbbing grew, and Tienne shuffled faster, his lips moving in exhortation. Both he and Morrie were perspiring freely now. Tienne's dark face gleamed. Morrie's features were contorted with his efforts on the drums.

Suddenly the drumming and chanting stopped, as if a door had slammed on them. Tienne sank into a chair. Wearily he took out his handkerchief and wiped his face. He bent forward and scooped up the white bundle. Gradually his face resumed its impassive mien.

The couples remained as they were, shaken and awed. There was something intangible vibrating in the air about them, retreating now.

Dave, panic in his eyes, gesticulated wildly and tried to talk, but no sound came. And, although the buzzing spectators may have thought for a moment that it was a joke, there was no mistaking the fright on Dave's face. Even Donna became concerned. Tienne got up and thrust his hand into his pocket, withdrew some leaves, and, crushing them between his fingers, massaged the powdered remains against Dave's throat. Dave burst into a torrent of words.

"I really couldn't talk! Did you think I was kidding? I thought someone had taken hold of my neck and squeezed." He grabbed Tienne by the lapel. "What did you do to me?"

"Just call it a form of hypnotism," he answered and shrugged Dave's arm away. For some time Tienne listened to the chorus of "How did you do it?" and "Show me how it's done," but finally he was able to work free of the press around him. The groups argued heatedly among themselves, forgetting him for the moment. When they looked for him later, he was gone. There were a few more drinks consumed and attempts made to renew the conversation, but the party soon broke up.

Carol sat quietly beside her husband in the taxi going home.

"That was quite a show Tienne put on—a new side to him. What did you make of it?" Roger asked.

"I—I don't know. It was all so bewildering. He has power."

"So did Houdini and Thurston," Roger said lightly.

"Don't laugh; I *felt* this."

"Agh, just sleight of hand, some new wrinkle of an old trick; there's probably a simple scientific explanation. As for Dave, anyone can hypnotize him when he's half stoned."

Should she tell him, Carol asked herself, about the little voice beating insistently against her eardrums during Tienne's chant—"I love you—I love you—you are mine—you are mine —" like a drumbeat? No! It would only reopen the wound made by that ugly scene only two weeks ago, just a few days after she and Roger were married. Roger had come home tired from his long hours of intensive lab work, to find her and Tienne laughing and listening to her records of little French songs.

"You just can't come here all hours of the day, Tienne, and visit with my wife when I'm not home," Roger had blurted. "We're married, and it's different now. Call it jealousy, but it doesn't look right."

Carol had been crushed, and Tienne retreated into his reserve. Never before had it been necessary for them to weigh their actions so carefully. Roger was tempted to end the strain with a jocular quip but decided it was better to have it understood from the beginning.

"Perhaps you are right," was Tienne's stiff reply. With a short "I'm sorry; I'll not trouble you again," he left, and they had not seen him until tonight at the party.

As a result of that showdown, Carol and Roger had had their first spat, although it was mostly hurt silence on her part. She was filled with compassion toward Tienne, but she could see Roger's point, also. But now she could never tell him of the poem—a poem of Tienne's—recited to her in a voice of quiet ardor in the university library:

> *"In the hills beyond Furcy*
> *The sky is blue and high,*
> *And the sea curls beneath our feet.*
> *My love will trust me;*
> *With her hand in mine*
> *We will soar with the eagles."*

And now, married, it was Roger and Carol who would soar with the eagles.

They had their tickets for a cruise of the Caribbean, including several days at Port-au-Prince. At Roger's hesitation at this part of their trip, Carol used her powers of persuasion, searching the depths of his eyes with her own pleading, serious look.

"Please—for friendship's sake—for Tienne's friendship with both of us. Remember how close we all were? He told me a long time ago a honeymoon in Haiti would be perfect. The fragrance of pine on the heights—the flowering poinsettia plants, tall as a man, blooming scarlet along the roads—I feel I know it. It should be especially beautiful this time of year, and he said the island will cast a magical spell around the heart. Please, for old times' sake?"

To further convince him, Carol added, "Remember when I moved from the apartment on Beall Street and you both helped? Will we ever forget the sight of Tienne walking down the sidewalk, with my bright dresses draped over one arm and a dozen books in the other, balancing my orange bed lamp on his head, with the cord tangling his legs?"

That brought laughter from both of them, and Roger gave in.

They sailed from Miami on a Thursday afternoon. Moving in an unbelievable sun-drenched world, the bright water and soft air beguiling them, they resisted the shipboard activities just to laze and relax on deck. At night the stars in the deep, dark sky winked at them as they stood catching a breeze and watching the phosphorescent wake.

Roger and Carol stepped out onto the dock at Port-au-Prince, into the melee that was Saturday on the Magic Island. At last, Carol thought,

the evergreen land that Tienne had praised so
gloriously! The waterfront and the city itself
teemed with vivid life and color. They went
through customs, showed their smallpox vac-
cination certificates. Roger barely had time to
check on their luggage, when Carol wanted to
know where she could shop for handbags.

"Later," Roger protested. "Later we'll have
time for that. Let's get to the hotel and freshen
up. I could stand a drink of that famous rum,
too."

They hailed a taxi and were off down Truman
Boulevard to the Grand Seigneur Hotel.

It was eight o'clock. Resting in their rooms at
the Grand Seigneur, they felt a delicious weariness after their tour of the city. No broken bones
were evident as a result of their careening rides
in the local camionettes and taxis, although tomorrow might show a few bruises. Surveying
the city and bay from the heights of Petionville,
they had descended to the museum to view the
anchor purported to be from Columbus' *Santa
Maria.* At Carol's urging, they had prevailed on
their slaphappy, suicide-bent taxi driver to take
them to the colorful Iron Market, where she had
run wild, purchasing a handbag, sandals, a
stunning hand-rubbed mahogany jewelry box—
and, best of all, a complete Haitian girl's costume. It consisted of apricot blouse, green skirt,

endless strings of bright beads, and a yellow, mannish straw hat with a broad orange brim.

When Roger lightly protested, she waved her hand laughingly. "Easy come, easy go. Don't be a Scrooge, darling; this stuff is really marked 'Courtesy of Fraser Oil.' " Then, half dreamily, "Wasn't it wonderful that they gave you that fat bonus for signing and time for this, too?" She waved out at the city and the sparkling bay.

Roger smiled indulgently. "We're not spending a whole month in Haiti—only four days. There are other places, after all. Besides, you know what Mr. Anker of Fraser Oil said. 'Take the month off for a honeymoon, and here's a bonus. But when you report for work, we're going to start taking our pound of flesh.' "

"Bosh!" She hugged him tight. "They know they hired a genius."

Roger held her close. "We're so lucky. Here we are, the girl from Ohio and the Nebraska boy, honeymooning in Haiti. I can't believe it."

"I know how you feel, darling. I have to remind myself twenty times a day, but won't it be fun telling our grandchildren about this?"

"Well, come on now, enough of this dreaming. Change, or whatever you are going to do. I'm going down to the bar and have a Barbancourt. That's real rum!" He paused at the door. "Say, about tonight—let's take in the night life at some of these cabarets. We'll eat at a good restaurant and make the rounds, okay?"

"Fine. Now shoo out of here. I'll join you in a few minutes, and maybe we can have a snack in the hotel dining room. I'm starved."

Later that night, at Buteau's, they sat at a little table in a secluded corner of the terrace, which afforded an excellent view. Carol was radiant in blue linen with white accessories. With casual crispness, it set off her shining hair and healthy, suntanned skin. As a concession to Carol, youth, and the tropics, Roger wore a flame-red dinner jacket. They ordered *langouste flambée,* the specialty, and found it delicious.

Laughing and talking honeymoon foolishness, they finished their meal and, leaving Buteau's, went on a round of the cabarets. They finally found themselves squeezed into a small club, with a minuscule table holding them apart. The insistent drumbeat, together with the flash and color of the place, brought home to them the exotic, vibrant life of the island. Carol's eyes were everywhere—so many laughing brown faces. Did everyone look like Tienne?

They ordered drinks and watched the sinuous dancing of the Haitian girl in the spotlight, a tall, bronze girl in a green and white dress and cerise turban. Her movements were liquid and languorous. She began to chant. The drums sank to a low throbbing, and the crowd quieted somewhat. At intervals, Roger caught the word "Malele."

"Carol, isn't that the same thing Tienne was saying at Dave Grayden's party? Remember it?"

"Why, yes, it does sound familiar."

Roger looked around. Almost sitting on their laps were a middle-aged couple, tourists from the States, like themselves. The man appeared distinguished, prosperous, and amused.

"Pardon me," Roger addressed the man, "but can you tell me what she is chanting?"

The man was glad to be friendly; he suggested they push their tiny tables together. He ordered another round of drinks. There were quick introductions.

"Strange that you should ask me," he told them. "Before we took our first trip, Betty and I boned up on Haitian history and especially on voodoo. We've been fascinated by it ever since. In this chant, she's seeking the help of Malele— the turnabout goddess—the capricious one. Malele is also called the 'Old One,' since one of her manifestations is in the guise of an old hag—a gray-haired crone."

"You called her capricious," Carol prompted.

"Yes," the man continued, "Malele is the only

voodoo goddess who can substitute herself for a real human being; then the spirit of the one she replaces is set free. For a favorite *houngans,* or voodoo priest, she can do this, but he must be powerful. Several times, back in the hills of Haiti, I understand it has been accomplished. But it always ends the same. First the victim disappears, then Malele—when she wishes." He laughed a little self-consciously.

Seeing the grave look on both the young people's faces, the man said, "Come, come, be gay! There's life and color and singing all about us. Don't take all this too much to heart."

Carol's gaiety increased, and Roger played along. They plunged headlong into the joyousness of the night. The couple, the Raddisons of St. Louis, stayed with them for a short time, but tired early and left.

In the late hours, they found themselves carried along in the colorful stream of traffic. It had been a hectic evening; their heads still throbbed with the beat of drums. They were bushed.

"Let's go back to the hotel," Roger suggested. "But first we'll get some honest-to-goodness bacon and eggs at the Saint Marc."

Carol nodded. "Then we'll call it a night."

They felt better, a little more clearheaded, after they had eaten, but when they got back to the hotel, they went straight to bed, weary but happy.

About an hour later, Roger woke. Aware of the subtle influence of the tropical night, he felt for Carol. She was gone. He got up and went into the next room, where a vague luminescence from some far-off light filtered in at the window. Carol was at the mirror, her face serene, as if she were asleep—or drugged. Yet her voice was plaintive as she argued softly with two shadowy figures in the glass. One was a squat, hideous old hag; the other a tall, handsome male Haitian. Tienne!

"Carol!" Roger cried, his voice hoarse.

The images misted, faded away, leaving the mirror blank. Carol lifted an indecisive hand to her forehead and shuddered, wrenching herself free from some bewildering embrace.

"Where—what am I doing here?" She fell into Roger's arms, sobbing almost soundlessly. "Hold me," she whispered. "I had a dream about Tienne and a horrible old woman."

"I know—I saw them."

"You saw!"

"Yes, curse him. This is Tienne's work."

His voice was angry and frustrated; he patted Carol's head, while many emotions fought within him. Then it hit him. He led her gently to a chair, then crossed over to a lamp and snapped it on. Next, he dragged out all their luggage.

It was in one of her small overnight cases that he found it, wedged cleverly between the blue satin lining and the outer shell, and when he pulled the small white bundle from its hiding place, the chicken bones and hollow sticks fell out and clicked upon themselves as they dropped to the floor. The few dirty white feathers drifted like snowflakes to the rug.

"How did they get in there?" Roger demanded.

Carol was bewildered for a moment, then her eyes widened in remembrance. "It must have been the night before we left! Tienne came over to say good-bye and to wish us luck, he said. I didn't tell you, for fear you'd be angry with him. I was packing and was in the room all the time —no! The phone call! It was to the travel agency, and I made it from Clarice's apartment across the hall because our phone was disconnected."

"That was it; that was all he needed to put that devilish thing behind the lining of your case. You see what he's doing, don't you? And he's on *his* ground!"

Roger's eyes lit with quick fury, then softened, and he said, "We'll get out of here first thing in the morning. Hang the rest of this trip! We'll fly back to the good old U.S.A."

Carol nodded dumbly and curled up against him, shivering.

"Let's go back to bed now, get a few hours' sleep, anyway," he said. "Things will look different in the morning." Exhausted, they fell into an uneasy sleep, her golden head resting on his outflung arm.

The air that drifted in at the window was laden with the fragrance of jasmine and mimosa. Outside, the tropical night held even the bird peeps in thrall. One, two hours crept by.

Then, downstairs, just before dawn, the heavy-lidded night clerk at the desk watched the last straggling revelers. He saw the blond girl cross the lobby. Dressed in Haitian girl costume of sisal shoes, bright apricot blouse, straw hat—strings of beads swinging—she opened the outer door as in a dream, her lovely face expressionless.

She paused a moment outside, then approached the ancient jeep parked at the curb. A proud young Haitian, his mouth wide in a gay smile, stood beside it and held the door for her. She got in.

"Where are we going?" she asked tonelessly, not looking at him.

He jumped in beside her, started the motor. Glancing down protectingly, he answered, "To the hills beyond Furcy."

The jeep chugged away.

Inside the Grand Seigneur, several floors up, Roger smiled faintly in his sleep, for the pressure of her head on his arm was reassuring. He gave an involuntary hug; nor did the stiff, scraggly gray hairs against his skin disturb his dreams.

ROBERT BLOCH

Floral Tribute

They always had fresh flowers on the table at Grandma's house. That was because Grandma lived right in back of the cemetery.

"Nothing like flowers to brighten up a room," Grandma used to say. "Ed, be a good boy and take a run over. Fetch me back something pretty. Seems to me there was doings yesterday afternoon near the big Weaver vault—you know where I mean. Pick out some nice ones and, mind you, no lilies."

So Ed would scamper off, climbing the fence in the backyard and jumping down over the old Putnam grave and its leaning headstone. He'd race down the paths, taking shortcuts through bushes and behind statues. Ed knew every inch of the cemetery long before he was seven; he learned it playing hide-and-seek there with the gang, after dark.

Ed liked the cemetery. It was better than the backyard, better than the rickety old house where Grandma and he lived; and by the time he was four, he played among the tombs every day. There were big trees and bushes everywhere, lots of nice green grass, and fascinating paths that wound off endlessly into a maze of mounds and white stones. Birds were forever singing or darting down over the flowers. It was pretty there, and quiet, and there was nobody to watch or bother or scold—as long as Ed remembered to stay out of the way of Old Sourpuss, the caretaker. But Old Sourpuss lived in another house, a big stone one, over on the other end, at the big cemetery entrance.

Grandma told Ed all about Old Sourpuss and warned him against letting the caretaker catch him inside the grounds.

"He doesn't like to have little boys playing in there," she said. "'Specially when there's a funeral going on. Way he acts, a body'd think he owned the place. There's nobody's got a better right to use it as they see fit than we have, if the truth was known.

"So you go ahead and play there all you want, Ed, only don't let him see you. After all, a body's only young once, I always say."

Grandma was swell. Just plain swell. She even let him stay up late at night and play hide-and-seek with Susie and Joe, behind the headstones. Of course, she didn't really care, because Grandma had her company over at night.

Almost nobody came to see Grandma in the daytime anymore. There were just the iceman and the grocery boy and sometimes the mailman—usually he just came about once a month with Grandma's pension check. Most days there was nobody in the house except Grandma and Ed.

But at night she had company. They never came before supper, but along about eight o'clock, when it got dark, they started drifting in. Sometimes there were only one or two, sometimes a whole bunch. Most always Mr. Willis was there, and Mrs. Cassidy and Sam Gates. There were others, too, but Ed remembered these three the best.

Mr. Willis was a funny man. He was always grumbling and complaining about the cold and quarreling with Grandma about what he called "my property."

"You have no idea how cold it gets," he'd say, sitting over in the corner next to the fireplace and rubbing his hands. "Day after day it seems to get colder and colder. Not that I'm complaining too much, mind you. It's nothing as bad as the rheumatism I used to have. But you'd think that they'd at least have given me a decent lining. After all the money I left them, to pick out a cheap pine job like that, with some kind of shiny cotton stuff that didn't even last through the first winter. . . ."

Oh, he was a grumbler, that Mr. Willis. He had a long, pale, old man's face that seemed to be all wrinkles and scowl. Ed never really got a good look at him, because right after supper, when they went into the parlor, Grandma would turn out all the lights and just keep the fire going in the fireplace. "We got to cut down on bills," she used to tell Ed. "This little widow's mite of mine is hardly enough to keep body and soul together for one, let alone an orphan, too."

Ed was an orphan; he knew that, but it never bothered him. Nothing seemed to bother him the way things bothered people like old Mr. Willis.

"To think I'd come to this in the end," Mr. Willis would sigh. "Why, my family owned this place. Fifty years ago it was just a pasture—nothing but meadowland. You know that, Martha."

Martha was Grandma's name—Martha Dean. And Grandpa's name had been Robert Dean. He had died a long time ago in a war, and Grandma never even knew where he was buried. But first he had built this house for Grandma. That's what made Mr. Willis so mad, Ed guessed.

"When Robert built this house, I gave him

the land," Mr. Willis complained. "That was fair and square. But when the city came in and took over—made me take a price for the whole shootin' match—there was nothing fair and square about that. Bunch of crooked lawyers, cheating a man out of his rightful property with all their gib-gab about forced sales and condemning. Way I see it, I still got a moral right. A moral right. Not just to that itty-bitty little plot where they planted me, but to the whole shebang."

"What do you plan to do?" Mrs. Cassidy would say. "Evict us?"

Then she would laugh, real soft, because all of Grandma's friends sounded soft, no matter how happy or mad they got. Ed liked to watch Mrs. Cassidy laugh, because she was a big woman, and she laughed all over.

Mrs. Cassidy wore a lovely black dress, always the same one, and she was all powdered and rouged and painted up. She talked to Grandma a lot about something called "perpetual care."

"I'll always be grateful for one thing," Ed remembered her saying, "and that's my perpetual care. The flowers are so pretty—I picked out the design for the blanket myself. And they keep the trim so nice, even in winter. I wish you could see the scrollwork on the box, too; all that hand carving in mahogany. They certainly spared no expense, let me tell you, and I'm mighty grateful. Mighty grateful. Why, if I hadn't forbid it in the will, I'll bet they'd have put up a monument. As it is, I think the plain Vermont granite has a little more restraint—you know, dignity."

Ed didn't understand Mrs. Cassidy very well, and besides, it was more interesting to listen to Sam Gates. Sam was the only one who paid much attention to Ed.

"Hi, sonny," he would say. "Come over and sit by me. Want to hear about the battles, sonny?" Sam Gates was a young-looking man, always smiling. He'd sit there in front of the fire, with Ed sprawled out at his feet, and then there would be wonderful stories to hear. Like the time Sam Gates met Abe Lincoln—not President Lincoln, but just plain Abe, the lawyer from down in Springfield, Illinois. Then there was the story about General Grant, and the story about something called the Bloody Corner, where the boys in blue really gave 'em the cold steel.

"Wisht I could have lasted out to see the finish," Sam Gates would sigh. "Course, by '64, wasn't one of us on either side didn't know how it would end. After Gettysburg we had 'em on the run. And maybe it's just as well I didn't have to go through all that messing around with Reconstruction, or whatever they called it. No, sirree, sonny, I guess I was lucky in a way, at that. Leastways, I never had to grow old, like Willis here. Never had to marry and settle down and raise a family and end up mumbling in the corner, trying to gum my pork chops. I'd have come to the same thing at the last, anyhow. Isn't that so, friends?" And Sam Gates would look around the room and wink.

Sometimes Grandma got mad at him. "Wish you wouldn't carry on that way," she'd say. "Watch your language, please. Little pitchers have big ears. Just because you're all sociable and come around on account of this house being more or less a part of the property—so to speak —that's no reason you got to go putting ideas in the head of a six-year-old. It ain't decent."

That was a sure sign Grandma was mad— when she said "ain't." And at such times Ed usually went out to play with Susie and Joe.

Thinking back, years later, Ed couldn't remember the first time he played with Susie and Joe. The moments they spent together were quite fresh in his memory, but other details escaped him—where they lived, who their parents were, why they only came around at night, calling under the kitchen window, "Oh, Ed-*deeee!* C'mon out and play!"

Joe was a black-haired, quiet kid of about nine. Susie was Ed's age, or even a little younger; she had curly, taffy-colored hair and always wore a ruffled dress, which she was careful not to stain or dirty, no matter what games they played. Ed had a crush on her.

They played hide-and-seek all over the cool, dark graveyard, night after night, calling faintly and giggling quietly at one another. Even now, Ed recalled how quiet the children were. He tried vainly to remember other games they played, like tag, where they'd touch one another. He was sure, somehow, that he had touched them, but no single instance came in recollection. Mainly he remembered Susie's face, her smile, and the way she called in her little-girl voice, "Oh, Ed-*deeee!*"

Ed never told anyone what he remembered, afterward, because afterward was when the trouble started. It began when the people from the school came and asked Grandma why he wasn't attending first grade.

They got to talking with her, and then they talked to Ed. There was a lot of confusion—he remembered Grandma crying, and a big man with a blue suit on came in and showed her a lot of papers.

Ed didn't like to think about these things, because they marked the end of everything. After the man came, there were no more evenings around the fireplace, no more games in the cemetery, no more glimpses of Joe or Susie.

The man made Grandma cry and talked about incompetence and neglect and something called a sanity hearing, just because Ed had been dumb enough to tell him about playing in the graveyard and about Grandma's friends.

"You mean to tell me you got this poor kid so mixed up that he thinks he sees them, too?" the man had asked Grandma. "That can't go on, Mrs. Dean—filling a child's head with morbid nonsense about the dead."

"They ain't dead!" snapped Grandma, and Ed had never seen her quite so mad, even though she'd been crying. "Not to me, they ain't, and not to him, nor to anyone who's friendly. I've lived in this house nigh all my life, ever since Robert was taken from me in that foreign war in the Phillypines, and this is about the first time a stranger ever marched into it—what you and your kind would call a living stranger, that is. But the others—they come around regular, seeing as how we share the same property, so to speak. They ain't dead, mister; they're just *neighborly* is all. And to Ed and me they're a darn sight more real than your kind ever was!"

But the man didn't listen to Grandma, even though he stopped asking questions and began treating her nice and polite. Everybody was nice and polite from then on—the other men that came and the lady who took Ed away on the train to the orphanage in the city.

That was the end. There were no fresh flowers every day at the orphanage, and, while Ed met plenty of kids, he never saw anyone like Joe or Susie.

Not that everyone, kids and grown-ups alike, wasn't nice to him. They treated him just so, and Mrs. Ward, the matron, told him that she wanted Ed to think of her as his own mother— that being the least she could do, after his harrowing experience.

Ed didn't know what she meant by harrowing experience, and she wouldn't explain. She wouldn't tell him what had happened to Grandma, either, or why she never came to visit him. In fact, anytime he asked any questions about the past, she had nothing to say except that it was best to try and forget all that had happened before he came to the orphanage.

Gradually Ed forgot. In the score of years that followed, he forgot almost completely. That was why it was so hard to remember now. And Ed wanted to remember, very badly.

During the two years in the hospital at Honolulu, Ed spent most of his time trying to remember. There was nothing else for him to do, lying flat on his back that way, and besides, he knew that if he ever got out of there, he'd want to go back.

Just before he went into the service, after getting out of the orphanage, he'd received a letter from Grandma. It was one of the few letters Ed ever received in his lonely lifetime, and, at first, the return address on the envelope and the name, Mrs. Martha Dean, had meant nothing to him.

But the letter itself—just a few scrawled and spidery lines written on ruled notebook paper— brought a rush of confused memories.

Grandma had been away, in a "sanotarium," as she put it, but she was back home now, and had found out all about the "put-up job they worked to get you into their clutches." And if Ed would like to come back home. . . .

Ed wanted very desperately to "come back home." But he was already in uniform and waiting orders when the letter came. He wrote, of course. He wrote all the while he was overseas and sent her an allotment, besides.

Sometimes Grandma's answers reached him. She was waiting for his leave to come. She was reading the papers. Sam Gates said it was a horrible thing, this war.

Sam Gates. . . .

Ed told himself that he was a grown man

now. Sam Gates was a figment of the imagination. But Grandma kept writing about her figments—about Mr. Willis and Mrs. Cassidy and even some "new friends" who came to the house.

"Lots of fresh flowers these days, Ed boy," Grandma wrote. "Scarcely a day goes by without them blowing taps over yonder. Of course, a body isn't so spry anymore—I'm pushing seventy-seven, you know—but I still get over for flowers, same as always."

The letters stopped coming when Ed got hit. For a long while, everything stopped for Ed. There was only the bed—and the doctors and the nurses and the hypo every three hours and the pain. That was Ed's life—that, and trying to remember.

Once Ed nearly told a skull doctor about the whole deal, but he caught himself in time. It was nothing you could talk about and hope to be understood, and Ed had enough trouble, without bucking for a Section Eight.

When he was able to, he wrote again. Nearly two years had passed, and the war was long since over. So many things had happened that Ed didn't even dare to hope very much. For Martha Dean would be "pushing eighty" by now, if. . . .

He got an answer to his letter a few days before his medical discharge came through.

"Dear Ed:" The same spidery scrawl, probably a sheet from the same ruled notebook. Nothing had changed. Grandma was still waiting, and she'd just known that he hadn't given up. But there was a funny thing she wanted him to know about. Did he remember Old Sourpuss, the caretaker? Well, Old Sourpuss was hit by a truck last winter, and ever since then he'd taken to dropping in with the rest of them evenings, and now he was friendly as could be, nice as pie. They'd have so much to talk about when Ed came back.

So Ed came back. After twenty years, after a new lifetime, Ed came back.

There was a long month in Honolulu, waiting for sailing—a month filled with unreal people and events. There were nights in a bar, there was a girl named Peggy, and there was a nurse named Linda, and there was a hospital buddy of Ed's who talked about going into business with the dough they'd saved up.

But the bar was never as real as the parlor back in Grandma's house, and Peggy and Linda weren't in the least like Susie, and Ed knew he would never go into business.

On the boat, everybody seemed to be talking about Russia and inflation and housing. Ed listened and nodded and tried to remember some of the phrases Sam Gates used to use when he told about Old Abe down in Springfield.

Ed took a plane from Frisco, wiring ahead to Mrs. Martha Dean. He got in at the airport in midafternoon, but he couldn't catch a bus for the last forty-mile ride until just before supper. He grabbed a bite to eat at the station and then jolted into town along about twilight.

A cab took him over to Grandma's.

Ed was trembling when he got out in front of the house on the edge of the cemetery. He handed the driver a five and told him to keep the change. Then he stood there until the cab drove away before he got up enough nerve to knock on the door.

He took a long, deep breath. Then the door opened, and he was home. He knew he was home, because nothing had changed.

Grandma was still Grandma. She stood there in the doorway, and she was little and wrinkled and beautiful. An old, old woman, peering up at him in the dimness of the firelight and saying, "Ed, boy—I declare! It is you, isn't it? Land, what tricks a body's mind can play. I thought I'd still be seeing a little shaver. But, come in, boy, come in. Wipe your feet first."

Ed wiped his feet on the mat, same as always, and walked into the parlor. The fire was going in the fireplace, and Ed put on another log before he sat down.

"Hard to keep it up, boy," Grandma said, "woman gets to be my age." She sat down opposite him and smiled.

"You shouldn't be alone like this," Ed told her.

"Alone? But I'm not alone! Don't you remember Mr. Willis and all the others? They sure enough haven't forgotten you, I can tell you that. Hardly talked about another thing but when you were coming back. They'll be over later."

"Will they?" Ed said softly, staring into the fire.

"Of course they will. *You* know that, Ed."

"Sure. Only, I thought—"

Grandma smiled. "I understand, all right. You've been letting the other folks fool you, the ones who don't know. I met a lot of them up to the sanotarium; they kept me there for nigh ten years before I caught on to how to handle them. Talking about ghosts and spirits and *dee*lusions. Finally I just gave up and allowed they were right, and in a little while they let me come home. Guess you went through the same thing, more or less, only right now you don't know what to believe."

"That's right, Grandma," Ed said, "I don't."

"Well, boy, you needn't worry about it. Or about your chest, either."

"My chest? How did you—"

"They sent a letter," Grandma answered. "Maybe it's right, what they said, and maybe it's wrong. But it doesn't matter, either way. I know you aren't afraid. You wouldn't have come back if you were afraid, would you, Ed?"

"That's right, Grandma. I figured that, even if time was short, I belonged here. Besides, I wanted to know, once and for all, if. . . ."

He was silent, waiting for her to speak. But she merely nodded, face bowed and dim in the shadows. At last she replied.

"You'll find out, soon enough." Her smile flashed up at him, and Ed caught himself remembering a dozen familiar gestures, mannerisms, intonations. Come what may, that was something nobody could take away from him—he was home.

"Land, I wonder what's keeping them," Grandma said, rising abruptly and crossing over to the side window. "Seems to me they're pretty late."

"Are you sure they're coming?" Ed could have bitten his tongue off a moment after he uttered the question, but it was too late then.

Grandma turned stiffly. "I'm sure," she said. "But maybe I was wrong about you. Maybe you ain't sure."

"Don't be mad, Grandma."

"I ain't mad! Oh, Ed, have they really fooled

you, after all? Did you go so far away that you can't even remember?"

"Of course I remember. I remember everything; even about Susie and Joe and the fresh flowers every day, but—"

"The flowers." Grandma looked at him. "Yes, you do remember, and I'm glad. You used to get fresh flowers for me every day, didn't you?"

She glanced at the table. An empty bowl rested in the center.

"Maybe that will help," she said. "If you'd go get some flowers. Now. Before they come."

"Now?"

"Please, Ed."

Without a word, he walked out into the kitchen and opened the back door. The moon was up, and there was enough light to guide him along the path to the fence. Beyond, the cemetery lay in silver splendor. Ed didn't feel afraid; he didn't feel strange; he felt nothing at all. He boosted himself over the fence, ignoring the sharp, sudden pain below his ribs. He set his feet upon the gravel path between the headstones, and he walked a little way, letting memory guide him.

Flowers. Fresh flowers. Fresh flowers from fresh graves. It was all wrong. It was Section Eight, for sure, but at the same time, it was all right. It had to be.

He saw the mound over at the side of the hill, near the end of the fence. Potter's field, but there were flowers on one grave; the single bouquet rested against a wooden marker.

Ed stooped down, scenting the freshness, feeling the damp firmness of the cut stems as he lifted the cluster from the marker. The moon was bright.

The moon was bright, and he read the plain block letters.

MARTHA DEAN
1870–1949

Martha Dean was Grandma. The flowers were fresh. The grave wasn't more than a day old. . . .

Ed walked back along the path very slowly. He found it hard to get back over the fence without dropping the bouquet, but he made it, pain and all. He opened the kitchen door and walked into the parlor where the fire had burned low.

Grandma wasn't there. Ed put the flowers in the bowl, anyway. Grandma wasn't there, and her friends weren't there, either, but Ed didn't worry anymore.

She'd be back. And so would Mr. Willis and Mrs. Cassidy and Sam Gates—all of them. In a little while, Ed knew, he might even hear the faint, faraway voices calling from under the kitchen window. "Oh, Ed-*deeee!*"

He might not be able to go out tonight, the way his chest was acting up. But sooner or later, he'd go. Meanwhile, they would be coming, soon.

Ed smiled and leaned back in the chair before the fire, just making himself at home. And then he waited.

YOU WILL ENJOY

THE TRIXIE BELDEN SERIES

28 Exciting Titles

THE MEG MYSTERIES

6 Baffling Adventures

ALSO AVAILABLE

Algonquin
Alice in Wonderland
A Batch of the Best
More of the Best
Still More of the Best
Black Beauty
The Call of the Wild
Dr. Jekyll and Mr. Hyde
Frankenstein
Golden Prize
Gypsy from Nowhere
Gypsy and Nimblefoot
Lassie—Lost in the Snow
Lassie—The Mystery of Bristlecone Pine
Lassie—The Secret of the Smelters' Cave
Lassie—Trouble at Panter's Lake
Match Point
Seven Great Detective Stories
Sherlock Holmes
Shudders
Tales of Time and Space
Tee-Bo and the Persnickety Prowler
Tee-Bo in the Great Hort Hunt
That's Our Cleo
The War of the Worlds
The Wonderful Wizard of Oz